"I don't want to talk about what happened sixteen years ago. I really don't."

He stuck his hands in his pockets, looked down at his boots and then up at her again. "We'll talk about other things, then."

"What things?"

"Anything. How you adopted your little girl." He said that gently. She almost smiled. But then he added in a low growl, "Or why the hell you married Nick."

As if he had any right to judge her choices. He'd left. What was it to him?

Folding her arms across her middle to keep from slamming her door in his face, she sternly reminded herself that it made zero sense to be so mad at him right now. They were nothing to each other. A memory. A love that wasn't strong enough, a love that didn't last.

So why did her heart throb painfully every time she saw him?

Dear Reader,

Most of us never forget our first crush, our first kiss... our first love. Rancher Jobeth Bravo never has.

Right after high school, Jobeth's first love, Hunter Bartley, left their hometown of Medicine Creek, Wyoming, to make a better life for himself. He wanted Jo to go with him, but she loved Medicine Creek and couldn't imagine living anywhere else.

Years later, she is long over him—or at least, that's what she told herself when her dad asked her if she would be okay with Hunter staying at the family ranch for a while. Turns out his successful home-improvement show is filming several episodes in town.

Jobeth reassured her dad that having her high school boyfriend living fifty feet from her front door would be no problem at all for her. What else could she say? But now he's right there on the ranch with her. And Jobeth is having to face the fact that she's not nearly as over Hunter Bartley as she thought.

Some of you may remember way back to the first Bravo family story, *The Nine-Month Marriage*, which came out in the late nineties. Jobeth was six years old then. She appeared in several Bravo books after that and I've had a lot of requests for her story. I kept meaning to get around to giving her the happy-ever-after she always deserved. At last, here it is.

And whether you're a fan of the Bravo family or a newcomer to the series, I hope this story sweeps you away and keeps you turning pages from the first chapter to the last.

Happy reading, everyone,

Christine

Hometown Reunion

———

CHRISTINE RIMMER

HARLEQUIN
SPECIAL
EDITION

Recycling programs
for this product may
not exist in your area.

ISBN-13: 978-1-335-72450-2

Hometown Reunion

Harlequin Enterprises ULC
22 Adelaide St. West, 41st Floor
Toronto, Ontario M5H 4E3, Canada
www.Harlequin.com

Printed in U.S.A.

Christine Rimmer came to her profession the long way around. She tried everything from acting to teaching to telephone sales. Now she's finally found work that suits her perfectly. She insists she never had a problem keeping a job—she was merely gaining "life experience" for her future as a novelist. Christine lives with her family in Oregon. Visit her at christinerimmer.com.

Books by Christine Rimmer

Harlequin Special Edition

Bravo Family Ties

Hometown Reunion

Wild Rose Sisters

The Father of Her Sons
First Comes Baby...
The Christmas Cottage

The Bravos of Valentine Bay

Switched at Birth
A Husband She Couldn't Forget
The Right Reason to Marry
Their Secret Summer Family
Home for the Baby's Sake
A Temporary Christmas Arrangement
The Last One Home

Montana Mavericks: Brothers & Broncos

Summer Nights with the Maverick

Visit the Author Profile page
at Harlequin.com for more titles.

This one's for Norma Carroll and her eighteen-year-old gray tabby cat, DC. Norma says DC is "kind of grumpy" and "carries socks around like he hunted them down and killed them."

When Norma's youngest child found him, DC was a kitten and barely weaned. At the sight of him, Norma's husband declared, "I don't want a damn cat." The remark reminded Norma of an old movie, a comedy mystery from back in 1965—and thus DC was named after the sleuthing Siamese in *That Darn Cat!*

Thank you, Norma, for sharing DC with me and allowing me to use his name and likeness to create the heroine's gray tabby in this book.

Chapter One

From the second-floor window of her sister's office at the *Medicine Creek Clarion*, Jobeth Bravo had an unobstructed view of the entrance to the Statesman Hotel.

As her little girl cooed happily in her arms, Jobeth stared at that entrance and thought of the past and wished she could change it somehow. Change it or let it go—forget it had ever happened. Wake up tomorrow morning, stretch and yawn and smile, and look forward to the coming day without the faintest remembrance of Hunter Bartley in her mind or her heart.

Starr, Jobeth's sister, glanced up from her desktop monitor. "Get away from that window." Starr frowned at the monitor again. "Hmm." Her fingers, swift and sure, went to work at her keyboard. As she typed some more on her next editorial, she muttered, "You are obsessed."

Jobeth didn't budge. She cuddled nine-month-old Paisley a little bit closer and continued to stare fixedly at the hotel across the street.

The Statesman was currently filled with reality-TV people from Hollywood. The TV people were in town to film several episodes of the hit home-improvement show *Rebuilt by Bartley*. No, Jobeth couldn't see a single one of those TV people right now. But she knew they were in there—not Hunter Bartley, though. The star of the show was bunking elsewhere.

"Da-ga-wa…" Paisley tried to stick a plump finger up Jobeth's nose.

"No, you don't." Jobeth caught her tiny hand. Paisley giggled as Jobeth said glumly, "I don't think I want to go home. Not for four months at least." Filming was expected to take that long. *Rebuilt by Bartley* would be renovating a bunch of different buildings in town. The whole thing was a very big deal, a series-within-the-series called *Hunter Comes Home*.

Starr beat out another burst of words on her keyboard and then remarked, "Please. It's not like he's going to be living in your house with you."

Jobeth nuzzled Paisley's dark baby curls and grumbled, "Close enough."

Due to the Hollywood invasion, as Jobeth chose to think of it, the Statesman Hotel had no vacancies. Also, Cottonwood Grove, the mobile home park at the south end of town, was chockablock with fancy trailers filled with members of the production crew. Still, there were other places to stay in town. Medicine Creek enjoyed a brisk tourist trade in the warmer months. The tourists needed places to stay. There were other hotels and a growing number of Vrbo and Airbnb rentals around town. And yet, her dad had offered to put Hunter up at the ranch and Hunter had said he would love that.

Why would he do that? As the star of the show, wouldn't he get first pick of available lodging? Why say yes to a bedroom in the Rising Sun Ranch house with a bath down the hall? The questions kept playing on a loop in her head.

Really. Why?

At least Jobeth had her own house—a house she loved that she'd built six years ago. Too bad that house was fifty yards from the main house.

"He'll be around." She continued staring out the window as she rocked her baby girl from side to side. "I'll be running into him. It's unavoidable."

The wheels on Starr's desk chair creaked as

Jo's stunningly beautiful forty-two-year-old sister rose to her feet. "You should have just told Dad no when he asked you if having Hunter around would bother you." Starr Bravo Tisdale was not only the owner and editor in chief of the *Clarion* now, but she was also eight months along with her third child, a surprise baby. With a groan, she rubbed at her lower back. And then, her giant belly leading the way, she joined Jobeth and Paisley at the window.

Jobeth shook her head. "It's been sixteen years. I've been married. He's been married. We were kids. It's not a big deal. I know this. I told Dad this."

"Awph!" Paisley leaned toward her aunt, chubby arms outstretched.

Starr caught her and gathered her close. "Then why are you so completely freaked out right now?"

Jo glared out the window. "I'm fully aware that I'm being ridiculous."

Starr responded gently, "I didn't say that."

"Of course, you didn't. I did. I really thought I could handle this." Hunter Bartley and the entire cast and crew of his popular show had arrived in town yesterday. "It's just that all of a sudden it's actually happening and I truly do not want to face him. He'll be at the ranch and I'm bound to run into him."

"It will be all right."

"No, it won't."

"Come on, Jo. It's just that you haven't seen him yet. Once you get past that first sight of him again you'll realize it's no big deal."

"Yeah?" Jobeth didn't say it, but she was thinking of Beau, Starr's husband. Starr had known Beau before he got sentenced to a couple of years at the state honor farm way back when. Beau had broken Starr's heart and seeing him again after he got out had been a very big deal for her. All that was decades ago. Now, Starr's heart was fully mended…by the man who'd once broken it. But Starr had to remember how it had felt to see his face again after the way he'd hurt her before.

"Okay." Starr shifted Paisley to one arm so that she could wrap the other around Jo. "I might be sugarcoating the situation just a little…"

"You think?"

"I'm only saying, you *will* be fine. You feel what you feel, Jo. Remember to breathe and don't beat yourself up."

"All these years…" Jobeth looked out the window at the brick facade of the old hotel. A fit-looking guy with a high-dollar haircut wearing tight jeans, dress boots and a leather jacket emerged from beneath the striped awning that framed the hotel entrance. *Not Hunter*, she thought as the stranger set off down Main Street. *Not Hunter, but obviously someone who works on the show.* She rubbed at the back of her neck in an effort to ease the tension that had gathered there.

Paisley let out another string of nonsense syllables and Starr chuckled at the sound.

Jobeth hardly heard them. She watched until the guy in the leather jacket disappeared from sight. "I never tried to find out how Hunter was, what he might be doing. Anytime I was the least bit tempted, I reminded myself to move on, let it go, leave the past alone." With a sigh, she confessed, "But now? Starr, I'm losing it." She met her sister's eyes. "The past few weeks, I've started stalking him online. What is wrong with me?"

"Nothing, Jo. Nothing is wrong with you..."

"So why do I feel like such a hopeless fool?"

"Come here." Starr pulled Jobeth closer, into an awkward hug that included both Starr's giant stomach and a giggling Paisley cradled between them. "You loved him, really loved him," Starr whispered. "Love is not a crime."

"Maybe not. But still, I feel like I did everything wrong and I'm about to come face-to-face with all the ways I messed up."

The morning cloud cover had cleared a couple of hours ago. The sky was baby blue. The day's high promised to reach a downright balmy sixty degrees.

Feeling pretty damn good about everything, Hunter Bartley drove his leased Ram 2500 into town with the windows down.

The pine-scented air blew in around him and the truck sailed over the rutted ranch road, hardly bouncing at all. On his way to a series of last-minute preproduction meetings in town, Hunter had the Bighorn Mountains in the rearview mirror and his hometown of Medicine Creek up ahead.

So far, being back where he came from wasn't half-bad, which thoroughly surprised him. Sixteen years ago, when he'd loaded his tools and the rest of his worldly possessions into his battered Ford Maverick and headed south, he couldn't wait to get the hell away from here. He'd needed to leave Medicine Creek behind and find a bigger life, one where he wouldn't forever be the poor, motherless kid with the loser father.

A low laugh escaped him. The past was just that. Gone.

These days, life was good. The rented truck had a great sound system and Chris Stapleton was currently singing "Starting Over" in that whiskey-and-gun-smoke voice of his. Hunter liked that song, so he ordered his Google assistant to turn up the volume. On the low, grassy hills to either side of the road, Rising Sun cattle lifted their heads to stare as he went by, his windows wide open, the music blaring good and loud.

He was singing along, beating out rhythm on the steering wheel, thinking about Jobeth, about all the years between then and now, wondering when he would finally see her again. Sooner or later, it would happen. For the next few months he would be spending his nights on the ranch where she lived.

As he topped the next rise, he spotted a cow in the center of the dirt road, directly in his path. "What the…?"

He stomped the brake. Tires spit up a rain of dust and gravel, and he jerked to a stop several yards from the animal.

You'd think the truck barreling toward her would have encouraged her to get out of the way. No such luck. "Google, turn the music down." Chris Stapleton faded to a low, husky rumble and Hunter stuck his head out his open window. "Git along, now! Go!"

The big red cow was not impressed. She stared and chewed.

He put the pickup in gear again and rolled forward nice and slow, figuring that would get her moving.

Nope. Tail flicking, she held her ground. He honked. She didn't budge, not unless you counted her tail and her left ear—the one with the tag on it. Both were twitching.

He laid on the horn.

The ear kept flicking and the cow kept chewing. Slowly, she turned her head his way. Now her big brown eyes were locked with his through the windshield.

Alrighty, then. A little extra encouragement was called for. After putting the pickup in Park, he climbed out and approached the cow. Stubborn to a fault, she remained in the center of the road.

At least she seemed like a calm one—maybe too calm. She let him get up close and personal without budging an inch.

She didn't even move when he caught her ear and peered at the tag. "So, RS-241, you are quite the rebel, I see." The bulging eyes regarded him with the wisdom of the ages. "Got nothing to say for yourself?"

Apparently not. He was about to give her a slap on the rump in hopes that would finally get her off the road when a second crew cab rolled to a stop on the far side of the cow. A woman in old jeans and a plaid shirt got out.

It took his stunned brain several seconds to register that the woman was Jobeth.

Damn, she looked good—slim and strong as ever, with that straight taffy-colored hair pulled back in a low ponytail. Those blue eyes were wide and solemn.

Older, yeah. But still the same Jo, with sweet, pale freckles sprinkled across the bridge of her nose and over both cheeks. The same Jo...

He had no doubt she still lived to get up before dawn on a frigid spring morning and go searching for newborn calves that had failed to get upright and latch on. Once or twice, back when they were together, he'd ridden out with her. She'd let him drive...

He remembered those times like they'd happened last week.

When she found a dying calf, she would hoist it into the cab on the passenger side and turn the heater on full blast to start warming the animal up. He would drive her and the calf to one of the barns, where she'd put the poor thing under a heat lamp. Once it came to life and struggled to its feet, they would load it in the pickup all over again and return it to where the bewildered mama waited.

"Hello, Hunter." She regarded him solemnly across the red back of the unmoving cow.

So weird. Otherworldly, even. This close in the early afternoon sun, he could see the faint beginnings of laugh lines bracketing her soft mouth and the first hint of crow's feet around those unforgettable aquamarine eyes. The signs of the passing years were barely discernable, but still, they kind of broke his heart all over again.

Because damn. It had been way too long.

He tipped the brim of his Dodgers cap. "Jobeth. Good to see you." And it was. Very good.

Her gaze scanned his face. "Got a problem?"

"Well, RS-241 here won't get out of the road."

She pulled a phone from her pocket and made a quick call. "Hi. It's me." She explained about the red cow and rattled off their approximate location. "Send one of the hands for her? Great. Thanks." As she stuck the phone back in her pocket, she turned to him again. "I'll just get her off the road and you can be on your way."

Completely enthralled, he watched her retreating backside as she jogged to her pickup. Returning with a length of rope, she fashioned a lead and slipped it over the cow's head. The cow followed without resistance as she led the animal to the shoulder, where she tied her to a fence post.

About then, Hunter started to worry she would simply climb back in her truck, swing around him and his vehicle and drive away. He jogged to meet her as she left the tied-up cow.

What to say to her? He had no idea. He just needed to get her to stick around a little longer. He wanted to look at her for a while, to listen to her voice. It seemed like yesterday that he'd left her behind…and yet, like forever, too.

She'd stopped walking as soon as he started toward her. Those eyes of hers, a luminous mix of blue, gray and green, watched him suspiciously.

He opened his mouth to say God knew what... and right then, from back in her pickup, a baby started crying.

What the hell? There was a baby? His gut hollowed out. Her dad had never said a word about a baby—not that Hunter had asked.

But still...shouldn't he have known if Jo had had a baby?

Okay, yeah. Now and then over the years, he'd gone looking for her online.

In the Facebook profile she rarely updated, he'd learned that she'd married Nick Collerby. She'd even posted their wedding picture. Finding out that she'd married Nick, of all people? That was a shocker. Back in school, she and Nick could hardly stand each other.

They hadn't made it work. He knew that because four years ago she'd changed her status to single again.

But really, he had no idea what she'd been up to relationship-wise since then. He slid a swift glance downward, at her left hand.

No ring.

Jo laughed. The sound got down inside him, burning, causing an ache that felt too much like yearning. "What are you looking at, Hunter?" she asked.

"Nothing."

"Right…"

Really, he'd done a bad job of stalking her over the years. He should have at least kept in touch with one old friend from town who might have passed on dependable information about her. But then, he never did have real friends back in the day. Only Jo. Jo had been everything.

And besides, the whole point was *not* to know. Not ever. Because he hadn't changed and neither would she, and there was nowhere it could go with them. He'd only trolled for her online in moments of weakness, when he couldn't stop thinking about what might have been.

The baby was still fussing. Jobeth stepped around him and headed for her pickup. Should he just let her go?

Damn right.

But he couldn't. In something of a trance, he followed.

She opened the back-seat door, leaned in and came out with a cute baby—a girl, judging by her pink fleece pullover embroidered with little white daisies. The pudgy kid, who had light brown skin and curly black hair pulled up into two short ponytails on either side of her head, stopped crying the minute she was freed from the car seat.

"This is my daughter, Paisley." Jo's face was tender, adoring. She cuddled the baby, who blinked her wide dark eyes at Hunter.

Bursting into an adorable smile that showed four tiny front teeth, two up and two down, the baby babbled a few random syllables and held out her little arms to him.

He almost reached back…but Jo gathered the baby closer and kissed her fat cheek. "She's nine months old. Babies are supposed to be wary of strangers at her age. Not Paisley. She thinks she's everyone's best friend. Don't you, sweet cheeks?"

The kid patted Jo's cheek. "Maw-maw-maw!"

He shouldn't ask. But he did. "So you're married, then?"

"No. I adopted Paisley when she was born."

Now he had a million questions— Can't you have children? Who's the birth mother? What about the dad? When did this happen? *Why didn't I know?*

He kept his mouth shut, barely.

And before he could figure out a way to keep her there, Jobeth had put the baby back in the car seat and handed her a big, bright plastic rattle that she instantly tried to put in her mouth.

Jobeth shut the door and turned to face him. "Well, good to see you, Hunter." Her eyebrows drew together. He realized she was waiting for him to step back, say goodbye. When he didn't, she added, "I'm heading on home." And then she was turning away from him, striding around the rear of her pickup to get up behind the wheel.

He remained in the middle of the road staring blankly after her as she drove away.

Jobeth's hands didn't start shaking until she'd left Hunter and his fancy crew cab behind. She clutched the steering wheel tighter to make the shaking stop and drove on. Her heart lurched against her breastbone, feeling heavy inside her chest, feeling all wrong.

So strange. She'd been calm and self-possessed while he was right there in front of her. But the moment she drove away, her heart had started pounding. A bead of sweat trickled down her temple. She lurched around one bend in the road and then another.

When she felt confident he wasn't going to turn his truck around and follow her, she pulled to the shoulder, shifted into Park and let her forehead droop against the steering wheel. Sucking in slow, deep breaths, she tried to calm herself down.

In the back seat, Paisley giggled and shook her rattle, oblivious to Jobeth's messed-up reaction to seeing her high-school boyfriend again.

It took several deep breaths and a lot of silent self-recrimination before Jo pulled herself together.

Okay, then. It had happened. She'd seen Hunter

again, at last. The experience had not been pleasant. But he'd been civil and so had she. Next time she saw him, it would be easier. Eventually, she would get so she could smile and wave and walk on by.

Dropping back against the seat, she lifted both hands. They weren't shaking anymore. So she put the pickup in gear and drove on toward the mountains that were still topped in mist and snow.

Her heart grew lighter as she turned off the ranch road and onto the circular driveway, which took her past the foreman's cottage and on to the Rising Sun's two-story main house.

In a classic farmhouse style, the ranch house had been built by her great-grandfather, Ross Bravo, almost seventy years ago now. It had a wide front porch with four tall double-hung windows on the main floor, two on either side of the door. It was a handsome house, she thought with pride.

Jobeth smiled when her mom came out the front door and ran down the steps toward her. Jo poked the button to open the passenger-side window and her mom leaned in.

Tess Bravo had curly dark hair and dark eyes, while Jobeth took after her light-haired, blue-eyed birth father, Josh DeMarley, who had died in an oil-rig accident when Jobeth was seven.

After Tess and Zach married, Zach had adopted

Jo. They were a true blended family. Her mom and Zach had had two sons together, Jo's half brothers, Ethan John and Brody. As for Starr, she'd been born to Zach's first wife.

In the back seat, Paisley threw down her rattle. It bounced on the floor mat as Paisley reached out eager arms to her grandmother. "Ga-ga-maw!"

"Shall I take her?" Tess asked hopefully.

"That'd be great. I want to check in with Dad, see what needs doing and maybe put Moonshine through her paces." A two-year-old Arabian mare, Moonshine was just adjusting to the saddle.

Her mom already had the door to the rear seat open to get the baby out. She scooped Paisley into her arms but left the big diaper bag there on the seat. Tess had all the baby gear she might need in the main house. She looked after Paisley often.

After shutting the back-seat door, Jo's mom stepped up to the front passenger window again. "You happen to pass Hunter on your way in?" she asked way too innocently.

Jo kept her expression carefully neutral. "Yes, I did."

"Everything…okay?"

"He had a little run-in with a cow but I handled the situation."

Tess blew a raspberry on Paisley's cheek and the baby snickered. "I was more wondering…" She let her voice trail away, probably in hopes that Jo would finish her sentence for her.

No way. "Wondering what, Mom?"

Tess's expression was both patient and resigned. "You don't want to talk about him."

No, she did not. "Love you, Mom."

Tess gave her a gentle smile. "Love you, too."

Jo leaned toward the passenger window and made a show of waving at Paisley. "Bye-bye…"

Paisley waved back and parroted her words. "Bye, bye, bye, bye…"

"I'll pick her up around five or so."

"Stay for dinner?"

"We'll see," she lied.

No, she would not be eating at the main house tonight. Hunter might show up. Yes, she needed to get used to having him around.

And she would.

Just not tonight.

With another quick wave, she drove on to her own house.

In town, Hunter visited the barnlike structure on Mill Street that the show's production company, Home Restoration Media, had leased as an office and meeting space for *Hunter Comes Home*. He checked in with his producer and the director, and stuck around for a couple of quick meetings. It was after five when he left the offices.

Before heading back to the Rising Sun, he strolled over to Main Street to visit the Medicine Creek Library. The library, basically a big brick box with multiple windows in front, had been built in the midnineties. It was one of the buildings the show would be taking on. The idea was to make it more open, more welcoming.

As he walked along Main, people waved at him and smiled—friendly smiles, too. They called out, "Hunter! Welcome home!"

He recognized some of them. It surprised him, how happy they all seemed to see him. He'd expected a different reaction, imagined resentful glances, or at least a little attitude, a clear display of their disbelief that good-for-nothing Esau Bartley's loser son had ended up a TV star.

Inside the library, with its tired gray carpeting, packed shelves and cramped seating areas, the first person he ran into was the head librarian, Mrs. Copely. She'd looked at least eighty sixteen years ago and hadn't changed a bit.

"Hunter Bartley!" she exclaimed in a whisper-shout, her wrinkled lips spreading in a pleased smile. "Look at you. Handsome as ever. It's so good to see you."

Had he somehow slipped into another dimension—one where Mrs. Copely treated him like visiting royalty? Should he have expected this? Maybe. But he hadn't.

Apparently, people became downright adoring when you planned to spiff up their run-down public buildings.

Mrs. Copely put her hand over her name tag and actually pantomimed a beating heart. "So proud," she said. "You've done so well, and now you're here in town to work your magic on our own Medicine Creek Library and our chamber of commerce, too." She babbled on in a thrilled whisper about how his "people" had worked a miracle, raising funding for the two community projects.

Hunter and his team, along with local construction crews, would also be rebuilding the bunkhouse out at the Rising Sun. They would renovate a gift shop and fix up Crystal Creek Lodge and Cabins at the foot of the Bighorn Mountains, just west of town. For those three private projects, the show and the owners would split the cost, fifty-fifty.

Mrs. Copely kept up her excited whispering. He didn't have to say a word. The woman told him how wonderful he was for ten minutes straight.

Hunter listened, baffled and bemused, as she went on about how she'd always known he would make a success of himself. "Always. And I always wanted to tell you so. But Hunter, you were such a guarded, wary boy. Back then, I never felt I would get through to you. I've always known I should have tried harder to reach out, though. I should have encouraged you not to let the difficulties of your childhood hold you back." She scoffed. "But who am I kidding? You hardly needed my encouragement. Because you *didn't* let your early troubles run your life, now did you? You have done so well—spectacularly, even."

In the end, before she let him go, she grabbed him in a hug. He breathed in her powdery, floral perfume and said how great it was to see her again, which wasn't exactly a lie. Who wouldn't find it gratifying to discover the librarian you'd always thought despised you hadn't hated you, after all?

A little dazed from all that admiration, he wandered down the street to another of the buildings slated for renovation—the gift shop, Amestoy's Treasure Trove.

At the sight of him, Carmen Amestoy stepped out from behind the counter and hugged him, same as Mrs. Copely had. She said she remembered how he'd kept his dad's business going when his dad was "under the weather."

Hunter hid a smile at her choice of words. Drunk on his ass as usual, that was his dad.

"You were just a boy," she said and patted him on the cheek. "But always mature beyond your years. We all hoped you would marry Jobeth—you two were always so devoted, after all…"

Devoted.

He supposed they had been. But not devoted enough to make it last.

By the time he left the gift shop, he'd started feeling as though he'd stepped into some alternate-universe Medicine Creek. A place that looked like his hometown but wasn't. A place where the past had been rewritten to make him a hero-in-training rather than a sullen kid whose mother had died when he was four—a kid who couldn't wait to get out of town.

If only his reunion with Jobeth had gone as well as his library visit and his conversation with Carmen Amestoy.

He drove back to the ranch thinking of Jobeth.

She hadn't seemed the least bit happy to see him that afternoon. And the minute she'd handled the issue with the cow, she'd jumped back in her truck and raced away, leaving him no opening to get her talking, no chance to suggest they maybe get a coffee in town or take a walk down by Crystal Creek, which ran in a lazy meander across the broad expanse of Rising Sun land.

And what about that baby? He still wanted to know what made a single woman decide to adopt a kid on her own.

Yeah. He really did want to spend a little time with her, to talk some more—not that it was a huge deal or anything. But they did have a lot of catching up to do.

No, he had no illusion that they would ever get back together. The break had been too painful. Too much time had passed. They were two different people now with completely different lives.

And yet, he did feel drawn to her.

Why shouldn't they take full advantage of this chance to get to know each other a little again?

Chapter Two

Catching up with Jobeth turned out to be easier said than done.

She didn't appear at the main house for dinner that night. He didn't run into her the next day. Or the next.

On Thursday morning, as he and two of Carmen Amestoy's grandsons were getting ready to knock out a back wall at the gift shop, Hunter's phone lit up. It was a local number he didn't recognize.

He went outside to take the call.

"Hello, Hunter. It's Starr Tisdale. How've you been?"

"Can't complain—good to hear from you."

She chuckled. "You're probably wondering how

I got your cell number…" He was hoping maybe Jobeth had asked Starr to reach out to him, but really, Jo could have easily gotten his number from Zach. No need to send her sister to coax it out of him. Starr added jokingly, "I'm the editor of the *Clarion*. I have my ways."

He'd always liked Starr. She was sharp, fearless and never failed to speak her mind. "Let me guess," he said. "Your dad gave you my number."

"Busted."

So then. Not Jobeth. He tried not to feel let down.

"Listen," Starr said. "I want to do a series of features for the *Clarion* about you Hollywood people invading our peaceful little town."

"You're not exactly selling it, Starr."

She laughed. "So, then. Yes, you're on board with getting a bunch of free publicity from the *Clarion*?"

He did want to get on her good side. Maybe she'd help him wrangle a little quality time with Jo. Plus, she was right. Free publicity was more likely to help than hurt.

"All right," he said. "I'm on board."

"Excellent. I'm guessing there's some producer I should talk to, and I want you to tell me who."

He gave her the names and numbers of the showrunner in LA and the on-site producer. "Tell them both I referred you."

"You know I will. You're a fine man, Hunter Bartley."

So tell me how to get Jobeth to talk to me. Somehow, he couldn't quite push those words out of his mouth. "See you soon, Starr."

"Thanks, Hunter."

"Anytime." He needed to make a damn move now or she would be gone. "Oh, and Starr…"

"Hunter…" She let his name trail off. The woman knew exactly what he wanted to know.

He made himself ask for it. "Give me Jo's cell number, will you?"

"You could just knock on her door."

"So that's a no, then?"

Starr rattled off the number. He pulled the carpenter pencil from behind his ear and wrote it on a bit of dusty Sheetrock he found at his feet. Starr added, "She's going to be pissed at me."

"Thank you."

"Don't mess it up, Hunter."

"I'll do my best."

"Later." And then she was gone.

Every spare moment he got for the rest of the day, he practiced what he would say when he used the number Jo's sister had given him. He never made the call, though.

He told himself it was because Jo would be out somewhere on the Rising Sun, maybe fixing a fence or feeding a bum calf. She would just say she had to go and that would be that. Better to catch her in the early evening after the day's work was through.

But then the evening came and went and he'd yet to make that call. He ate at the ranch house with her family…but she wasn't there.

The next day, Starr showed up at the library during taping. Jobeth's sister was hugely pregnant and gorgeous as ever. The producer, Melanie Huvey, called a five-minute break to introduce the newcomer, and then Starr took a chair and started typing away on a laptop.

Hunter planned to approach Starr casually, to chat her up a little, try to get her talking about Jobeth. But they were taping a sequence where he consulted with Mrs. Copely and the members of the library board. That meant he was on camera and yakking his face off nonstop. He didn't get a break for a couple of hours. When he finally had a free moment, Jo's sister was gone.

That evening, he stayed in town to eat. It was getting too depressing, eating with the Bravos every night. Jobeth had not come to the main house for dinner one time since he'd moved into the guest room upstairs. That wasn't like her. He knew because when he first came to town, both Zach and Tess had mentioned that Jo ate with the family a couple of times a week. He should probably take the hint that she wanted nothing to do with him.

She'd moved on and had no desire to see him or talk to him.

At Arlington's Steakhouse, he sat at the bar and ordered a stiff whiskey and a T-bone. He was sipping his drink and wondering why he couldn't seem to either give it up with Jobeth or make a real plan to get some time with her, when Melanie Huvey took the stool next to him. The producer asked the bartender for a vodka cranberry juice and then said to Hunter, "Starr Bravo."

"Was that a question?"

Mel grinned like a shark. "She's gorgeous, smart and articulate. I like her. Tell me everything."

He put his phone away. "Down, girl. She's married."

Mel sighed. "Yeah. I saw the ring. And it looks like she's having that baby any day now. I want to get her on tape." Beyond renovating the five properties, they were intercutting brief interviews with interesting or prominent local people—the mayor, the circuit judge, someone from the chamber of commerce—in addition to the usual scenes with the owners and employees at the reno sites.

"Starr's a good choice," he said. "She's not shy and she knows how to handle herself."

"The hot, pregnant lady journalist." Mel nodded thanks as the bartender delivered her drink.

"I love it." She leaned closer to Hunter. "How do you know her, really?"

"You know the answer to that. She's Zach Bravo's daughter."

"Right. And you were really close to the other daughter, Jobeth, before you moved to LA."

"How do you know that?"

"I ask a lot of questions. Sometimes people answer me honestly. Am I right about the other daughter?"

"Mel. What are you getting at?"

The producer braced an elbow on the bar and propped her chin on her hand. "I've been conferencing with Terry." Terry Sloane, who'd remained in LA to run his Home Restoration Media empire, was the creator and executive producer—aka, the showrunner—of *Rebuilt by Bartley.* "We still need at least one or two more of the people you grew up with—relatives, running buddies. An old flame would be fabulous." Mel was still grinning.

He grinned right back at her and said pleasantly, "Not going to happen."

"Which?"

He had two uncles, their wives and some cousins in town, but there'd been a falling-out between his dad and his uncles back when Hunter was still in elementary school. At this point, he barely knew his uncles or his cousins, and he wasn't sure he was ready to just pick up the phone and give them a call.

Running buddies? He'd had none. As for an old flame…

He could hardly see Jobeth agreeing to share the juicy details of their high-school romance on a home-improvement show—not that he would want her to.

Mel prompted, "The house painters you suggested are named Bartley." *Rebuilt by Bartley* hired local companies to do the renovations whenever possible. For this project, they'd asked him for a list of any Medicine Creek companies he remembered and would recommend. His uncles had been the best. He'd discovered from their website that his cousins ran things now, so he'd put them on the list.

And no way was he sharing his complicated, painful family history with Mel.

She knew it, too. "You're looking reluctant, Hunter," Mel accused. "Terry warned me you would be." Hunter kept his mouth shut. She added, "At least we have Zach Bravo. We might get a few fun tidbits from him, from that lovely wife of his and from Starr, as well."

Terry had suggested a bunkhouse rebuild as one of the projects for *Hunter Comes Home*. Hunter had thought of Zach, who'd always been good to him. And then memories of Jo had flooded his mind. He'd said he would contact Zach before he allowed himself to consider the idea more logically.

And then Zach had surprised him and said yes. He'd started thinking that getting together with Jo again, kind of touching base in a casual way, wouldn't be that big of a deal.

Until he'd arrived in Medicine Creek, met Jobeth on the way into town and knew just from the look on her face at the sight of him that she wanted to get as far away from him as possible. Now he wanted to reach out to her more than ever. But he felt unsure of how to do that…or if he even should reach out to her.

What was his damn problem?

He wanted to spend some time with her. And he wasn't shy with women. He'd dated a lot when he'd first gotten to LA. He'd been married and divorced. Since the divorce, he'd dated some more. Sophisticated women, glamorous women. He'd recreated himself when he moved to LA. Now, he never had trouble talking to anyone. If he wanted to get close to a woman, he found a way to get a damn conversation going with her.

Mel patted his arm again. "Did I lose you there, Hunter?"

"Of course not." And hadn't he gotten enough

of this crap from Terry, who'd kept after him for months now about needing more of his "history," his "roots" in town? "I'll give it some thought," he said.

Mel had to know he was blowing her off, but she didn't take offense. "Good." She gestured at the table by the window, where the director and the production coordinator were already seated. "Join us."

"Thanks, but I'm waiting on a call." Waiting on himself to make the damn call, to be specific.

Mel grabbed her drink and headed off to join the others. Hunter ate his steak and left.

As for his call to Jobeth…

Didn't happen that night, either.

Or over the weekend.

Another week went by. That Thursday, Starr's first article about the show appeared in the *Clarion*. It was charming and folksy and funny. People in town loved the publicity and so did Terry and Mel.

As usual, Hunter was putting in long days on the project, constantly checking on construction crews at all of the five locations and also making time for filming as each project inched along. The library, the chamber of commerce, the gift shop and the lodge had all opted to stay open with shorter hours and some reduction in service during the renovations. That meant extra work for the construction crews. They would be managing the teardowns and rebuilds in stages, masking off work areas in each building, trying to keep the construction noise to a minimum.

Customers and patrons didn't seem to mind the disruption at all. Carmen Amestoy claimed her shop had gotten busier since the work started. Her customers loved dropping in to see what the Hollywood people were up to.

The days flew by. The nights went on forever.

On the second Tuesday in May, he was up well before dawn.

Ranch people got up good and early, too. He found Jo's mom, Tess, in the kitchen with Edna Heller, whose daughter, Abby, was married to Zach's cousin, Cash Bravo. Years ago, Edna had been the housekeeper on the Rising Sun. Now she lived in the foreman's cottage, which was a short walk from the main house. She and Tess were very close and had been as far back as Hunter could remember.

"Coffee?" Tess asked him.

"I'll get it." He took a cup and sat down at the big kitchen table with Edna, who asked how all the TV people were holding up living in hotels and trailers in the wilds of Wyoming.

"So far, so good," he replied, and answered more of Edna's questions as Tess fried bacon on the big stove. Soon, Zach and their younger son,

Brody, would come in hungry from early chores. Hunter could smell the biscuits baking in the oven.

He'd always liked the ranch house, the homey smells, the kindness of the Bravos. They were a real family, all wrapped up together, looking after each other, knowing they could count on each other.

"Eggs, bacon and biscuits, Hunter?" Tess sent him a quick smile over her shoulder.

His stomach growled in response. "Yes, please."

"Set yourself a place."

He knew where everything was—same drawers and cupboards as back when he and Jobeth were together, when he spent more time in this house than he did in the cramped, dark cabin west of town where he lived with his drunk dad. Tess fixed him a plate. The food was delicious, as always, and he told Tess so.

Too soon, it was time to head into town. He cleared off his place and thanked Jo's mom.

He was just about to turn for the door when Edna said, "Since you've been staying upstairs we don't see much of Jobeth."

An electric jolt shot up his spine. Edna's voice had sounded teasing—like she was challenging him to take a chance, make some kind of move.

Two weeks had flown by since that day on the road when he and Jobeth faced off over the wide back of the uncooperative red cow. Two weeks, and every minute of that time, he'd felt Jo's resistance, a wall of silence pushing at him, keeping him out, holding him away.

He'd been telling himself for months now that reconnecting with Jo again might be nice if it happened. He'd reminded himself that she might not want anything to do with him, and if she didn't, well, that would be fine. That spending time with her was no big deal either way.

Now he realized the truth. Not only did she want nothing to do with him, he'd been lying to himself.

He wanted to spend some time with her, to get to know her again. He wanted that a lot.

And yet, he'd done practically nothing to make it happen. Every time he reached for his phone to call her, he stuck it back in his pocket and told himself to respect her wishes, to keep away.

But come on. One awkward meeting in the middle of the road did not a rejection make.

There was a hunger inside him, to talk to her. To spend time with her. To hear from her lips everything she'd been doing the past sixteen years.

He even wanted to know about her marriage to Nick—how it had come about, and how it had ended. Jobeth and Nick…

They made zero sense. They'd never really gotten along.

He looked directly at Edna, who had to be eighty now. Her hair was a silvery nimbus around her delicate face. She had a Betty White vibe about her, a pretty older lady with a will of iron and a sharp sense of humor. "Jobeth seems busy," he said. "Real busy. Every time she catches sight of me, she has somewhere else to be."

The lenses of Edna's frameless glasses twinkled as she smiled. "Catch her when she can't just walk away."

"Evenings are a good time," Tess offered quietly. "She puts Paisley to bed around seven, so after seven is best. She'll be home for the night. You might just knock on her door, ask her how she's been all these years."

Warmth filled him to think that Tess and Edna would give him a nudge in the direction he wanted to go. "After seven. I'll do that, thanks."

"Don't ring the doorbell," Edna advised. "Knock quietly, or you might wake the baby."

He grinned all the way into town. It meant a lot, that Tess and Edna seemed to be rooting for him to pull it together and make his move.

Jobeth had just put Paisley to bed and walked into the front hall when someone knocked on the door. It was a quiet knock. Probably her mom.

Her pretty wrought-iron front door had iron-work glass on top. She could have easily peered out to see who was waiting on the other side. But it had been long enough since those few moments on the ranch road that it didn't even cross her mind it might be Hunter.

By then, she felt reasonably certain he wouldn't be making much effort to interact with her again, so she pulled the door wide, expecting to see her mom. And there he was in faded jeans and a coffee-colored bomber jacket.

Butter soft, that jacket—she could tell just from looking at it. Lambskin, no doubt. The wind stirred his thick dark hair. He looked like what he was now—someone easy in his own skin, someone confident. Someone with the money for thousand-dollar lambskin jackets and fancy haircuts. "Uh. Hunter. Hi."

Those velvet-brown eyes locked with hers. "Starr gave me your number, but after the way you looked at me that day with the cow, I was scared to call."

"So you knocked on my door instead."

He nodded. "Your mom and Edna said this time of night was a good time to maybe get you to talk to me."

Starr, Edna, her mom. All of them so willing to help him connect with her. They all thought the world of him, just like her dad did. Just like everyone in town did.

Not that they shouldn't think highly of him. He *was* a good guy. Even after he'd ripped out her heart, she'd known he was better than he'd ever believed himself to be. But that didn't mean she wanted to spend an evening staring at his too-handsome face while taking a long stroll down memory lane.

She said, "I don't want to talk about what happened sixteen years ago. I really don't."

He stuck his hands in his pockets, looked down at his boots and then up at her again. "We'll talk about other things, then."

"What things?"

"Anything. How you adopted your little girl." He said that gently. She almost smiled. But then he added in a low growl, "Or why the hell you married Nick."

As if he had any right to judge her choices. He'd left. What was it to him?

Folding her arms across her middle to keep from slamming her door in his face, she sternly reminded herself that it made zero sense to be so mad at him right now. They were nothing to each other. A memory. A love that wasn't strong enough, a love that didn't last.

So why did her heart throb painfully every time

she saw him? And why did she want to punch him in the face for mentioning Nick in that mean, dismissive tone.

"You got married, too," she accused. "Some important producer named Lauren Maris, right? She was how you got your big break, wasn't she?"

His eyes didn't waver. "Let me in. I'll tell you anything you want to know."

She stared down at her sheepskin house boots. It wasn't that cold out—low fifties, maybe. But the wind was up a little. A gust of it blew in through the open door, swirling around her, stirring the hairs at her nape. She shivered.

Why wouldn't he just give up and go?

"Come on, Jo. It won't kill you to look at me."

She lifted her head, met his eyes and made herself speak more reasonably. "It just seems pointless. I mean, it can't go anywhere. We both know that. We've always known it. Just like before, you will go and I will stay. That's who we are. It feels wrong to get into it with each other."

"Who said we had to get into it—or that it had to go anywhere?"

Once again, he had it right. It *didn't* have to go anywhere. It didn't and it wouldn't. He knew that. She knew that. And yet, she'd just *had* to make a point that it wouldn't. And that made her feel foolish and petty. The way she was acting, you'd think she'd never gotten over him. "I, um…"

"We were everything to each other." He said it softly, sincerely. Her heart melted a little. "And we were kids. But since then, we've grown up. It seems to me that, after all this time, we ought to be capable of making peace with each other, of getting along."

He was right for the third time in as many minutes. She needed to be better than this, stronger. Less angry. Kinder.

But every time she met his eyes, bitterness slithered through her.

"Come on, Jo. We have to start somewhere. I'm going to be living in the main house for months."

She gritted her teeth. "I'm aware."

"Think about it. You can't race off like your hair's on fire every time you catch sight of me. And it's not right that you haven't been over there for dinner with your family since I arrived. I feel bad about that. I said yes to your dad's invitation to stay here at the ranch because he said you were fine with it."

She made herself admit the truth. "Because I told him I was fine with it."

"But you don't act like you're fine with it." Okay. Now she really felt like the bad guy here.

He asked, "Do you want me to move into town, is that it?"

She opened her mouth to say yes.

But that would be unfair. It was over, the love they'd had. It was over and it was years ago. He'd wanted her to go away with him and all she'd wanted was for him to stay.

She'd seen his going as a betrayal. And standing here tonight, facing him across the threshold, she had to admit the truth to herself. She'd never let go of her fury that he'd left her, that he'd chosen his longing for a different kind of life over her.

But hadn't she chosen her life on the Rising Sun over him?

It was time she got over thinking like a self-absorbed eighteen-year-old girl. She was the one who'd been behaving badly since he returned to Medicine Creek. She needed to stop that. She needed to get used to having him around.

He seemed like a decent man, he really did. A decent man who'd behaved more bravely, more honestly, than she had these past two weeks.

Shame moved through her, heating her cheeks, knotting her belly.

She needed to get over herself, let the old hurts go. It was the only way to make things better. The two of them might even come to a kind of peace

with each other. And peace would be good, a defi-
nite step in the right direction.

Could they actually be friends?

That seemed a little far-fetched.

But at least they could be honest with each other.
They could find a way to get along with each other
for the months he would be living in her parents'
house.

"Well?" he prompted. "Do I get to come in?"

She stepped back and gestured him forward.

Chapter Three

Hunter really liked her house. "You built yourself a barndominium," he said when she led him into the open living area.

A barndominium was all-metal construction, even the framing. And these days, with lumber at a premium and intermittent supply-chain issues, buyers of new homes often waited months for the lumber to be available so that construction could begin. With a barndominium, you didn't have that problem.

She gave him a nod. "I love it. It's twenty-five hundred square feet all on one floor—both energy-efficient and low-maintenance."

"It's beautiful," he said. "And it gives me ideas.

We need to feature one on the show, maybe as an add-on to a traditionally constructed home." On *Rebuilt by Bartley*, the point was always to repair, improve and upgrade an existing structure.

Right then, a gray tabby cat peeked out from behind the big sectional sofa. It strutted right to him and wound around his legs. "Is this...?"

"DC." At last, Jo granted him a smile. "You'd better believe it." She'd named the cat after the sleuthing Siamese in the movie *That Darn Cat*— the original Hayley Mills version made way back in the 1960s. She'd told him once that her dad had loved that movie as a kid and bought her a DVD of it back when she was ten or eleven. Jo had always idolized Zach. And she'd loved *That Darn Cat* as much as her adoptive father did.

He picked up DC. "How've you been?" DC regarded him stoically. "Still Mr. Personality, I see." He nuzzled the old guy and then scratched him on the head. "Wait. I think that might be a purr..."

"Don't bet on it. He's as cantankerous as ever."

When they were together, they used to joke that DC had been a cranky old man from birth.

The cat squirmed. Hunter set him down and he trotted off toward the kitchen island. "How old is he now?"

"Eighteen." DC had been born to one of the barn cats. When the mama cat disappeared, Jo had taken charge of feeding the kittens. She'd found homes for all of them, except the aloof, grumpy one. She'd named him DC and kept him for herself.

They were staring at each other. He didn't want to look away. "Long time ago," he said, his voice low, a little rough.

"Yeah…" She seemed to shake herself. "Coffee? Or something stronger?"

"Got a beer?"

She got one for each of them and they sat on the comfy, oversize sectional.

"I don't even know where to start," she said a little breathlessly. Her smooth eyebrows scrunched up as she frowned. "Not with the exes, if you don't mind."

He did mind. He wanted to know everything that had gone down with her and Nick—the how and the why and the what-were-you-thinking?

However, right now he was in no position to start making demands. "Will you tell me about your little girl?"

She sipped her beer. "What do you want to know?"

"Well, you adopted her, you said. Tell me about that."

"All right. I wanted a baby, wanted to start my own family, though I'm single now and likely to stay that way."

Why? What happened? I need to know every-

thing. It wasn't easy, but somehow he kept his mouth shut.

She set her beer on the coffee table. "I considered the options—a sperm bank, adoption. An adoption from an agency was likely to be difficult. They give priority to married couples. So I was kind of settled on trying intrauterine insemination to start.

"But then the daughter of my mom's cousin in South Dakota became pregnant. She was in her senior year of high school. She had a full ride to a great college in the fall. She and the birth father weren't together anymore. Neither of them felt ready to raise a child. So we arranged an independent adoption. I was there when Paisley was born and I brought her home with me a few days later."

He had a million questions. Did the birth mother stay in touch? Had Jo met the birth father?

Every question he might ask seemed too personal, somehow—too personal and none of his business. At least at this point, anyway.

She studied his face. And then, as if she'd guessed his thoughts, she said, "Paisley will know about her birth parents. And she will have the option to seek them out when she's eighteen. Both of the parents signed off all rights, however."

"But you're open to them being in her life if they change their minds?"

"How could I not be?" She looked so sad then. Sad, and yet determined.

He wanted to reach for her, grab her close, press his lips into her hair, reassure her, somehow.

But he had no right to do any of that. So he asked the next question. "You said you're single and likely to stay that way...?"

She hitched up her chin. "Yes, I am."

"You don't think you'll ever get married again, then?"

She sat up a little straighter and gave a one-shoulder shrug. "I'm not looking for a man and I didn't want to wait around for the right guy to show up."

What could he say to that one? "Makes sense." And it did, he supposed.

"So glad you approve." She was on to him. That look in her eye said she knew he was only saying what he thought she wanted to hear. A lock of hair had come loose from her topknot. She guided the strands behind her ear.

He let his gaze run over her, thinking how, after all this time, he still liked everything about her. The pride and the starchiness. Her strength and her independent nature. And damn, she looked good in old jeans, a long-sleeved Wyoming Cowboys T-shirt, UGGs on her feet and zero makeup on her face.

"My turn," she said.

"Go for it."

"Well, Hunter, you couldn't wait to get away from here when you left."

Not from you, Jo. Never from you. "It's true."

"What made you come back?"

He considered giving her the whole truth. But he was only just now admitting that truth to himself. It was too soon and too risky to share that truth with her. "Hometown shows are big right now. Terry Sloane, the creator of my show, wanted to get on that train. He approached the network with the idea of choosing four or five locations in *my* hometown and giving each one an episode, making it a series within the series. The network signed on. Everyone agrees that *Hunter Comes Home* has a real nice ring to it."

"But what about you? When you left, you swore you'd never be back."

"And I meant it…then. You might remember that I was a bitter kid."

"Yes. I do remember…"

"But years have gone by. I've done all right. I don't feel all that bitter anymore. Still, when Terry first pitched me the idea, my knee-jerk reaction was a flat no."

"And yet, here you are."

"You'd have to know Terry. He views the word *no* as a challenge to his powers of persuasion. He kept after me. I started admitting to myself what a great idea it was—and please don't freak out, but I did want to see you again." The words seemed to escape of their own volition, though he'd reminded himself two minutes ago not to say them.

She went completely still and asked flatly, "Why?"

He went ahead and told the plain truth, or at least, a good portion of it. "To make peace with you, I hoped. To do what we're doing right now. Catching up, maybe eventually putting the past behind us." She was sitting way too straight. He blew out a hard breath. "I'm sorry. Too much, too soon, huh?"

She shifted uncomfortably. "Well…"

"I'm freaking you out. Admit it."

"No. Honestly. I'm not sure where this is going, but I'm not freaking out."

"Good." They shared a silence, one full of tension and all the things that remained unsaid. He went on with his list of reasons for coming back to Wyoming. "And then there was the look-at-me-now angle."

She actually grinned. "I get that."

"Yeah. I planned to walk around town and smirk at everyone who ever looked down on me, rub it in their faces that I'd turned out to be more than just the town drunk's loser son, after all."

"They didn't look down on you, Hunter."

"Yeah." He said it gently. "You used to tell me that."

"And you never would listen."

"I was messed up," he confessed.

His mom had died of a burst appendix when he was four. His dad couldn't deal with losing her.

Esau Bartley always claimed he'd started drinking the day he lost his darling Anna. *Started that day*, Hunter's dad used to mutter to himself, slurring the words, shaking his head. *Started that day and never gonna stop...*

Jo's soft mouth had thinned to a hard line. "I'll say it again. Nobody ever blamed you for your dad's problems, Hunter."

Esau had worked as a handyman. Until Anna died, he'd been good at his job...or so everyone always said, including Hunter's grandmother, Daisy, who had loved him and looked after him until she, too, died. He was eleven by then.

He remembered there had been visits from Social Services. His dad had pulled himself together for a while. He'd cleaned up his act enough that Hunter never got put in the system.

Hunter was still eleven when he started helping his dad. By the time he was sixteen and already deeply in love with Jobeth, his dad had grown scarily undependable.

Esau was always losing jobs because he just didn't bother to show up. By then, Hunter was doing most of the work himself. It was better that way. He didn't really trust his dad with a saw or a drill. Esau could have hurt himself too easily—not on purpose. Just from being too out of it to care.

But his dad didn't die from an injury on the job. He died because he went fly-fishing while drunk. Before dawn on a chilly morning in May of Hunter's senior year, Esau waded out into Crystal Creek, got swept off his feet and drowned.

Hunter thought of Mrs. Copely at the library, of Carmen Amestoy, of all those friendly, smiling faces so happy to see him back in town. Not one of them had seemed especially surprised at his success.

"What is going through that brain of yours?" Jo demanded.

She used to ask him that question all the time, when he would grow quiet thinking of the dark cabin, pretty sure that when he got back there his father would be passed out drunk on the couch surrounded by half-empty takeout containers, full ashtrays and an empty bottle or two.

Really, looking back at the screwed-up kid he'd been once made his heart hurt, like a big fist had grabbed it and put on the pressure.

He busted himself. "I'm thinking that you were right, that's all. Mostly right, anyway. There were a few people who did look down on me." Including her ex-husband, he thought but didn't say. "It wasn't the grown-ups," he added. "Just some of the kids." They would give him a hard time for not having the right clothes and never getting a haircut.

She sighed. "The jerks, you mean."

"Right. But overall, no one blamed me. I was just too messed over to realize it back then."

She looked stricken when he said that.

And maybe they'd gotten too honest, too fast.

But sitting here with her again, at last, after all this time, he felt like nothing had changed. He still knew her to the core.

And right now he knew just from looking at her that something was breaking her heart.

He asked warily, "What's the matter? What'd I say?"

She drew a slow breath. "I used to think that someday you would wake up and see that people did understand—that they admired you, even, the way you did your best in such awful circumstances, the way you tried to help your dad any way you could. I thought when that day came, I would have to stop myself from rubbing it in your face that the people in this town weren't so bad, after all."

"But now you don't want to rub it in my face?"

"No, I don't. Looking back now, I see that I didn't want to admit how hard it was for you. I mean, your dad wasn't violent or anything. He never said mean things to you."

"No, he never did."

"And you were always so capable. I thought you should just accept that you really were handling your problems. I thought you should be able to pat yourself on the back and put all the crap at home behind you. I never wanted to admit how awful it must have been for you to go home to a father who wasn't really even there. How scared you had to be, that something would happen to him and you would have no one—I mean, that's why you needed to leave. Medicine Creek had too many hard memories. You needed a new start. I see that now." She gave a laugh that skirted the razor's edge of pain. "Better late than never, right?"

Damn, he thought. This. Right now. It was what he'd missed the most since he'd been gone. Jo, telling it like it was. Looking him right in the eye and speaking the hard truth.

He had never, in sixteen years, stopped missing her.

He would probably be missing her for the rest of his life.

And he really needed not to think about that right now. Better to focus on the sad subject at hand. "My dad wasn't a bad man. He just didn't want to live in this world without my mom."

For that, he got a slow nod. She said, "I'm sorry that it was so rough for you growing up, sorry that I wasn't more understanding. I should have been.

Especially given my own life in the years before my mom and I came to Medicine Creek..." Her eyes were far away, suddenly.

Hunter knew she was thinking of her birth dad, Josh DeMarley, who'd been a dreamer, always looking to make it big. They'd lived paycheck to paycheck, moving from place to place, deeply in debt, barely getting by.

Jo blinked the past away. Her beautiful smile bloomed wide. "But I'm really glad you can finally admit that nobody in Medicine Creek felt anything but admiration for you."

He couldn't let that stand. "Come on. Nick never liked me all that much."

Her smile fled. "Maybe we're getting in a little too deep here." A moment ago, he'd thought so, too. But really, nothing had been said that didn't need saying. She reminded him flatly, "I thought we agreed not to talk about the exes."

"Sorry. But I have questions. Lots of them."

"Don't, okay?" She glanced away, scowling. "Just don't."

What do you know? His beer was empty and he'd already worn out his welcome.

He teased, "You're not going to offer me another beer?"

"Would you take it?"

"No."

She was nodding. "Same rule as always, then?"

"That's right." As the only son of a stone alcoholic, Hunter had never allowed himself more than one drink per day—and yeah, he and Jo were underage back then, but there was always a bottle of something passed around at a party or a keg at a bonfire out by Magpie Lake.

And she still wasn't meeting his eyes.

Yep. Time to go. He stood. "Thanks for letting me in. Finally."

She got up and followed him to the door.

He turned before he went out. "So now…"

She drew her shoulders back, as though steeling herself for a blow. "What?"

"No more running away the minute you spot me?"

For that, he got one of her looks—he remembered them all so well. The tender looks. The secret ones, just between the two of them. The chiding looks when she thought he couldn't even see what was right in front of his own damn face.

Now, she looked obstinate. Determined. "We're not friends."

"But we could be."

"Hunter, we hardly know each other anymore."

Liar. He didn't say it out loud because he didn't want to lose what little ground he'd gained with her. "Just, you know, stop and say hi. Show up to dinner at your folks' house so I don't feel like it's my fault they hardly see you since I moved in."

She wrinkled her nose at him and swiped that stray lock of hair back behind her ear again. "I see them every day."

"But they miss you at dinner. The way I heard it, you and your little girl ordinarily eat with your family at least a couple of times a week."

"Who, exactly, did you hear that from?" She tossed her head and that shiny swatch of hair escaped yet again.

He wanted to be the one to smooth it back and that meant he had to concentrate good and hard on keeping his hands to himself. "Sorry, Jo. It wouldn't be right for me to rat out your family members."

"But you have discussed me with my family. That *is* what you're saying."

She was gearing up for an argument. Nothing that came out of his mouth right now would tip the scales in his favor. So he just looked her square in the eye and kept his mouth shut.

By some miracle, she backed down. "Fine." She gave him what he'd always thought of as her royal look, like a queen granting a small kindness to a humble peasant lad. "Paisley and I will have dinner at the main house."

"Great." He just couldn't let it go at that. "When?"

It surprised the hell out of him when she replied, "Tomorrow. How 'bout that?"

He was scheduled for a working dinner with Mel and the show's director, David Reid, tomorrow. Too bad. Mel and David could wait. "See you then."

"How's she doing?" It was her father's voice.

Jobeth glanced over her shoulder as Zach came toward her. Still ruggedly handsome in his early sixties, Zach had blond hair and blue eyes, same as Jo's birth father. Nowadays, people who hadn't been told never had a clue that Jobeth wasn't Zach's biological daughter. Sometimes even Jo forgot.

He joined her just outside the open door to the stall. His dog, Winston, a handsome blue heeler, dropped to his haunches a few feet away and surveyed the action through alert brown eyes.

In the stall, the laboring mare was lying on her side, softly snorting, letting out the occasional drawn-out groan.

"She's doing really well," said Jobeth. Eight years old and delivering her third foal, the pretty spotted mare, Freckles, was easy-natured and mellow. "Water's broken. We'll be seeing the real action any minute now…"

The last time Freckles foaled, her baby presented in the wrong position, and it was not a breach Jo and her dad could turn themselves. They'd had to call the vet. This time, Jobeth had decided to be extra careful. The past few days, she'd given instructions that the mare should be put in the horse barn at night and checked on at regular intervals.

Restless after the surprise visit from Hunter, Jobeth hadn't slept much that night, anyway. When her phone lit up with the message that Freckles was foaling, she'd been lying there wide-awake, thinking how ridiculous it was that her high-school boyfriend could still keep her awake at night all these years later. She'd called her mom to come and keep an eye on her sleeping baby and headed for the horse barn.

Now, it was after one in the morning.

"Honestly, Dad. You didn't have to get up."

"I wanted to." He smiled, his craggy features blurry in the red light from above. Calming to horses at night, the red light reinforced circadian rhythm.

"Here we go," whispered Jo as Freckles expelled a hard huff of breath and another gush of fluid. The small front hooves, still covered by the birth sack, peeked out. The foal's head appeared next, all smashed down on the spindly front legs.

"Never gets old," her dad whispered.

Some horse owners got right up on the mare when she foaled. They touched and fondled the foal at birth under the theory that such imprinting created a bond between the foal and the owner, establishing a relationship of security and trust.

Jo and her dad left birthing to the mare unless a problem arose. They agreed that the foal's relationship to the mare was what mattered at this point.

So far tonight, the process had gone well. Freckles panted and groaned, shifting as if to try to stand and then flopping back to her side as she pushed. More fluid spilled.

Twenty minutes after the front hooves appeared, Freckles gave yet another hard lurch. That did it. The little one slid out, onto the thick bed of straw. Already, the baby's wet head had poked through the birth sack, though the rest of the bony little body remained covered in the wet veil of membrane. Freckles struggled to a standing position, the birth cord severing, the sac splitting and collapsing.

Her foal, a spotted filly, struggled to get her sticklike legs working properly as the mare nipped and chuffed at her. Finally, the little one staggered upward and stayed there, wobbling. The mare nibbled and nudged at her some more. In time, the little one latched on.

Jo and her dad shared a glance of satisfaction that the birth had gone so smoothly.

She said, "I think we're good here if you want to get a few hours' sleep." She would stay until the mare had expelled the placenta and she could treat the umbilical stump. It never hurt to keep an eye on mama and baby for a while longer.

Zach gave her a fond smile. "Nah. I'll stay."

They ended up walking back to the houses together as dawn paled the sky to the east. Behind them, Winston panted happily as he herded them along.

Halfway to the main house, Zach said way too casually, "We don't see you at dinner the past few weeks."

Jo bit the corner of her lip to keep from saying something snippy. She reminded herself that only her dad would come out in the middle of the night when he really didn't have to, just so he could wait for the right moment to broach a touchy subject—the subject of Hunter. And she kept trying to tell herself it was nothing, no problem, but at the same time she had carefully avoided being anywhere Hunter might be.

She slanted her father a quick glance. He was facing straight ahead. She couldn't see his eyes in the shadow of his hat. "Hunter stopped by my place last night right after I put Paisley to bed. I'm guessing Mom told him that was the best time to get me alone."

Zach nodded. "He might have gotten a little advice from Edna, too."

That didn't surprise her in the least. "Right."

"You have a good talk with him, then?"

"I gave him a beer. We caught up a little."

"And that's good, right?"

Was it? She still felt much too unsettled when it came to the grown-up version of the boy she'd once loved with all of her heart and soul—loved and lost and had a really hard time getting over.

She stopped walking and turned to face her dad directly. "It's been harder than I thought it would be, having him around."

Her dad put his weathered hand on her shoulder. "Be honest. Would you rather he found somewhere else to stay while he's here?"

Jobeth sighed and hung her head. "Dad. It's fine."

"You don't behave like it's fine."

"He always loved it here on the ranch. He had no use for Medicine Creek, but I do believe that his memories here, on the Rising Sun, are good ones."

"Well, I hope so."

"I do not want him to have to leave because I'm some delicate emotional flower who can't buck up and deal."

"Jo, I never said any such thing about you."

"Of course, you didn't. And it's all worked out, I promise you. Last night, he offered to move into town. I told him no way. I also told him I would come to dinner with the family tonight."

"Good." Zach pulled her close. For a moment, she rested her head on his shoulder. She breathed in his scent of dust and saddle soap, and thought how grateful she was that he'd found love with her mom and they'd made a family, the three of them and Starr at first, with Ethan and Brody coming along a little later.

At their feet, Winston, eager to be moving on, let out a whine. Zach loosened his hold.

They kept walking past the main house to her place. Inside, DC was stretched on the kitchen floor looking bored with the world and everyone in it. Her mom had Paisley in the high chair. "Maw-maw-maw!" the baby squealed in greeting and then stuck a wad of corn puffs in her mouth. Jobeth quickly washed up at the sink and went to give her little girl a kiss.

DC rose and strutted off toward the living area while Winston stretched out next to Paisley's high chair so he could scarf up bits of cereal as they dropped.

Tess kissed Jo's cheek. "Coffee's ready."

Zach took a turn at the sink. Jo poured the coffee and set the table as her mom whipped up some eggs and toast.

While they ate, Jo gave her mom a rundown on the uneventful birth. Tess generally named the fillies. "I'll get out and have a look at her and figure out what her name should be."

It took Tess until they were clearing the table to bring up the subject of how much they all missed having Jo with them at dinner now and then.

Jo shared a glance with her dad and Zach said, "We talked about that."

"Ah," said Tess. "Good. And...?"

Jo tried not to roll her eyes. "Tonight, Mom. I'll be there for dinner tonight."

That night, the family sat down to eat at six. Around the table were Jo, Tess, Zach, Edna, Brody and Paisley. Ethan John, twenty-four now, had his own place in town.

Very casually, her mom mentioned that Hunter had called. "He said he had a dinner meeting at Arlington's Steakhouse with people from his show and he couldn't get out of it."

Jo had been nervous about seeing him tonight, about sitting at the table with him, the family looking on. It should not have been a big deal.

Yet somehow, it sure had felt like one. She'd worn her hair down and spent way too much time settling on a ginger-red maxi dress with a pretty tiered skirt.

And now he wasn't even going to show up.

She told herself that she felt relieved he wasn't there.

It was a lie. She felt let down, pure and simple. Really, her emotions were all over the map. Was she having an early midlife crisis?

She needed to get a grip on herself.

As soon as the meal was over, Brody jumped up and helped clear the table, after which he announced he needed to head into town for "study group."

Seventeen and a junior at Medicine Creek High, Brody got up every morning before dawn to help with early chores. This weekend, he would work with Jo, her dad and the hands, moving cattle to fresh pastures. Brody got good grades, played baseball and football and had a girlfriend he was wild about, Alaina Kent. Jo suspected "study group" would consist only of him and Alaina, and way more canoodling than schoolwork.

"Back by ten," said Zach.

"Right, Dad." Brody sounded mildly annoyed, but he didn't argue. He grabbed his keys and headed for his F-150 pickup.

Edna had baked a coconut cake. Jo poured the after-dinner coffee and said yes to a slice.

They talked of Freckles' foal, which Tess had christened Dot. Jo had spent an hour with Freckles and Dot that afternoon. Freckles trusted both Jo and Zach. The mare stood by calmly while Jo petted and rubbed Dot, scratching her behind the ears, beginning the process of getting the little filly comfortable with having Jo in her space.

"She's a sweet baby girl," said Zach, who had also spent some time with the foal and her mama that day.

After the cake and coffee, Jobeth loaded the dessert plates and mugs into the dishwasher. By then, it was half-past seven. "Dinner was so good, and I think it's about time I put Paisley to bed."

Tess had Paisley in her lap. "I never want to let

loose of her," she said, laughing as Paisley tried to stick her plastic rattle into her grandma's mouth.

Jo had the wildest urge to suggest, *Why don't you just keep her overnight*? She knew her mom would jump at the chance.

And maybe Jo would head on into town, have a little *me* time, get a drink at Arlington's…

Her mom stared up at her with a sly smile on her face as Paisley shook her rattle and made nonsense sounds. "Honey, what in the world are you thinking?"

Mind your business, Mom. Jo almost said that right out loud.

Really, what was wrong with her tonight? She felt all prickly, out of sorts. "It's past Paisley's bedtime." She scooped the baby off Tess's lap.

Tess shook her head. "That is not what you were thinking."

"You callin' me a liar, Mom?" Jobeth asked in a teasing tone.

Her mom's smile softened. "Never—but anytime you want to leave her with me for an evening, you know you only have to ask."

She leaned down and whispered, "Love you, Mom. You're the best."

"Love you, too."

At home, Jo got the baby ready for bed and rocked her for a bit. Paisley fell asleep in her arms and didn't even stir when Jo put her in her crib.

A few minutes later, she stood in her family room with the big-screen remote in her hand, oddly reluctant to surrender to another evening of Netflix or HBO Max.

She needed…more.

Her life was good, full. She loved everything about the way things had worked out for her. She had her baby and her family, her own house on the Rising Sun. It was everything she'd ever wanted.

Almost.

"Argh." She groaned at the ceiling. Why wasn't she over this love thing yet? After all, she'd tried love. Twice.

The first time, the love she had was everything she'd ever dared to dream it might be. And then Hunter left.

With Nick, it was…less. She'd really wanted to make it work, to build a good life with him, to start a family.

But the whole thing was doomed from the start.

She flopped down into her favorite leather chair, hoisted her stocking feet onto the ottoman, tugged her long skirt over her legs and tossed the remote on the coffee table.

Maybe a bubble bath and a glass of wine would help her relax, get her past this weird, antsy feeling she had crawling under her skin. Maybe she just needed…

Someone knocked on the door.

Her heart started racing. She put her fingertips

to the side of her throat. Her pulse was going a mile a minute.

The knock came again.

She rose and went to answer, careful this time to peer through the glass at the top of the door before pulling it open.

It was Hunter, staring right back at her, one dark eyebrow lifted, waiting for her to let him in.

Chapter Four

Chapter Four

"Hi." Hunter tried to be lowkey and relaxed, though he wanted to fist-pump and shout, Yeah! when she answered the door. "I got stuck in a meeting," he said, loving the look of her, all boho in a long red dress printed with wildflowers, her hair loose on her shoulders. She'd probably worn boots with that dress but taken them off when she got home after dinner. Red cable-knit socks peeked out from under the hem of the skirt.

She stepped back without a word. He entered, then she shut the door behind him and led him into the family room.

"Have a seat," she said. "What can I get you?"

"Not a thing." He dropped to the big sectional.

She took the leather chair across the sofa table. "What's up?"

"I wanted to see you."

She gathered her legs to the side. Settling the skirt over her stocking feet, she leaned an elbow on the chair arm. "About what?"

Everything. Nothing. How the hell should I know? "My producers keep asking for interviews with people I grew up with…"

She wasn't going for it. "No way. Never. That kind of thing is not for me."

"You sure?"

Her stick-straight hair shimmered in the light from the wrought-iron lamp by her chair. "Absolutely positive."

He wanted to kiss her so damn bad. "They did ask me to ask you."

She shifted, turning her legs to the other side, and fussed with her skirt. And then she narrowed her eyes at him and accused, "You told them about me."

"Nope. I didn't say a word. But somebody did. It's a small town, Jo."

"No kidding."

"Everybody knows we were pretty much inseparable all through high school."

She drew in a deep breath and then nodded. "I would probably put my money on Carmen Amestoy. She always used to ask me if I ever heard from you. I would play it really cool and just say I had no idea where you were or how you were doing—which was the truth at the time. You weren't famous back then."

"Carmen's a nice woman," he said.

"Yeah." She was fiddling with her skirt again. "She has a big heart."

"And a mouth to go with it." They laughed together at that. He wished she was sitting on the sectional with him and not all the way across the coffee table in that big chair. "It's a renovation show, Jo. Rated G all the way. If you agreed to an interview, they wouldn't get too personal. They're hoping for some humorous insights into what I was like back in high school. And then for you tell them how much you love the plans for the renovated bunkhouse."

She was shaking her head.

He said, "Still not going for it, huh?"

"I would be too nervous and you never know what might come out of my mouth. I might say things you don't like and then where would we be?"

"I'm not worried. I have a great agent. That means there's a clause in my contract that says they have to edit out any personal information I don't want to share with the world of home-improvement TV."

"Well, that's good, but the answer's still no." She looked off toward the fireplace and the big screen above it.

He stared at her profile and felt a little bit guilty for wasting her time with this discussion. He'd already made it very clear to Mel that Jobeth would not be appearing on the show. Because he'd known Jo wouldn't go for it and he respected her privacy. But he'd needed to keep her talking until he was ready to make his move.

The goal tonight: to get her to go out with him.

She was looking at him again, suspicion in her eyers now. "Okay. What's going on with you?"

"Let me take you to dinner—Arlington's or the Stagecoach Grill." The words were out before he could stop them. He knew immediately that he'd blown it. Mentally slapping himself upside the head, he waited to get shot down.

But then she asked, "When?" The question had him blinking in disbelief. And she saw him do it. A sweet laugh escaped her. "Gotcha," she whispered, wrinkling that pretty freckled nose.

Damn. He wanted to kiss her.

Just once…to start.

But he kept his butt on the sofa and his hands to himself as he suggested ultracasually, "Friday night, then?"

"Okay."

Wow. Just like that. He could hardly believe his ears. "Great."

"And Hunter, they should interview Starr. She's good at stuff like that."

"Oh, don't worry. They will. They love her."

"Of course, they do. My sister is not only gorgeous, smart and unstoppable, she's a shameless *Clarion* booster. If it's good for the newspaper, she's on it."

"I noticed." He just sat there, staring at her, wondering if he was suffering from some sort of delusion. "You just said yes, right? Dinner with me. Friday night."

"I did, yes."

"The baby...?"

"No worries. Paisley will have a sleepover at her grandma's Friday night. Her grandma will be thrilled."

He had no idea what to say next. Dinner with Jo. After all these years...

He couldn't stop himself from asking one question, though... "What made you say yes?"

Her cheeks turned pink beneath the scattering of freckles. "I've been thinking, that's all."

"About?"

"About what you said. We both know where we stand. Just like before, you will be leaving and I will be staying. But that doesn't mean we can't spend a little time together while you're here."

* * *

Friday, Jo took Paisley out with her all day. She had an old play yard in one of the barns and used that, alternating with putting Paisley in a baby carrier and even letting her crawl around in clean straw for a bit when she needed a little freedom.

No, Jo didn't get as much work done as she did when she left her baby with Edna or her mom. She mostly stayed close to the barns and sheds, only venturing farther out when her dad needed help delivering a breech calf. She left Paisley in her car seat with the pickup's back doors wide open while she and her dad worked to turn and pull that calf.

At five, Jo took the baby to the main house.

Tess greeted her at the door. "Gimme that little sweetie." Jobeth handed her over.

Paisley giggled with happiness. "Ga-ga-ma!"

"I missed you today. Kiss?" Tess puckered up. Paisley laid one on her and Tess nuzzled her ear, then whispered, "We're having a sleepover, baby girl." Paisley replied with a flood of happy gibberish after which Tess stepped back and asked Jo, "Coming in?"

"No. I need to clean up."

"Have a good time." Tess's eyes twinkled. She knew Jo was having dinner with Hunter. Given that it was likely to get back to the family, anyway, Jo had just gone ahead and told her mom about their date. Now, Tess was trying really hard to mind her own business. "I'm glad you and Hunter are reconnecting after all this time."

Jo let a nod be her reply. "I'll pick her up first thing tomorrow."

"No rush. You know that."

After a last kiss on her baby's soft cheek, Jo returned to her own house, where she showered, applied light makeup and put on a short turquoise dress with her favorite boots, which were tooled in a pattern of twining flowers.

The whole time she got ready, she debated with herself, alternately asking herself what she thought she was doing—was she just begging for trouble by going out with Hunter again?—and then arguing right back that she had nothing to get all worked up about.

She and Hunter weren't those two teenage kids they used to be. They both knew where they stood. They had no illusions, no silly dreams of love forever after. It was a good thing to hang out with him now, a good thing to enjoy a little time with him, time free of bitterness and impossible expectations.

Or so she kept telling herself. However, when the doorbell rang, she was kind of a wreck.

"I can't believe we're doing this," she announced, breathless, as she pulled open the door.

"You look great," he replied, low and rough, those sexy brown eyes scanning up and down her body.

He looked good, too—so good—all in black with a braided silver chain around his neck, his beard so short it almost qualified as scruff and his sable brown hair trimmed close at the sides, but thick and wavy on top.

She was so busy thinking "no wonder he's got two and a half million followers on Insta" that she hardly realized he had one hand behind his back.

But then he whipped out a gorgeous bouquet of white roses and lavender. "Oh, you didn't…"

"You always liked the smell of lavender."

She took it from him and buried her face in the clean scent of her favorite flower. "I'll just stick these in water," she said when she lifted her head.

He followed her into the open central room. "Is Tess watching the baby?"

"Yeah." She got down a pitcher, filled it from the tap and put the flowers in it. "They are gorgeous. Thank you." She set them in the center of her big farm-style table.

When she turned, he was right behind her. They shared a smile as warmth curled through her. He was looking at her kind of strangely.

"What?" she asked.

He lifted a hand, slowly, like he was afraid if he made a sudden move, she might spook and run off. She stared up at him and her breath caught in her chest as he traced the line of her hair along the curve of her cheek with his index finger, his touch warm, slightly rough.

Ordering her lungs to draw in air, she thought about kissing him, about sixteen years going by without the perfect press of his lips against hers. It had been forever since she'd felt his kiss.

And she ought to just grab him close and plaster her mouth to his. She ought to kiss him until the past was forgotten and tomorrow didn't exist. Until there was only this moment—until neither of them could see straight.

He leaned in a fraction. Her mind swam. She felt ridiculously giddy.

Something batted her leg. She blinked and looked down. DC stared up at her.

Hunter glanced down at him, too. "You're cramping my style, cat." Looking smug, DC walked away. "He always was a troublemaker."

She chuckled and he met her eyes again. Winged creatures fluttered around in her belly.

And then he whispered, "We should go."

"Yeah. Let's go."

"If we don't, I'll probably grab you and kiss you."

She shook herself out of the trancelike state she'd somehow fallen into. "Can't have that." Drawing her shoulders back, she headed for the front door.

The hangers in the foyer closet jangled together

as she took out a light jacket. He plucked the jacket from her hand and helped her into it as she breathed in the scent of him, so woodsy and warm. She caught a glimpse of his watch, big and fancy with a chunky metal band, a bold blue face and more than one dial on the front, the kind of watch James Bond might wear…or maybe an astronaut on a trip to the moon.

She found him a little disorienting now, really. He was the boy she'd known, but not. He seemed so sure now, smooth in a way he never used to be. Calmer. And so much more confident.

None of that surprised her, given where he'd been and how well he'd done for himself. It did, however, make her feel at a loss, somehow, unable to keep up. Thrown back to the past as she stumbled around in the present.

Anchoring her small, multicolored leather cross-body bag on her shoulder, she pulled open the front door and ushered him out.

Neither of them said a word as they drove toward town. He had music playing, so not talking seemed okay. She felt a little awkward, but he didn't appear the least bit nervous or concerned.

Leaning her head back on the cushy leather headrest, she pictured them sitting at a table at Arlington's, rehashing old times, all pleasant and civilized. Or maybe just making small talk.

"Do you have a reservation at Arlington's?" she asked.

He sent her a quick smile. "Yeah."

"Cancel it."

"Sure," he replied without hesitation, then told his phone to call Arlington's. Two minutes later, he ended the call. "Now what?" he asked.

"Let's go to Mustang Sally's." The dive bar just outside the town limits had been open for business since long before either of them was born. "We'll get a burger, play darts maybe, just generally hang out."

Hunter couldn't decide whether they were doing something interesting, or their date had just derailed.

But he didn't ask questions. He wanted to be with her...and wherever that took them, he was willing to drive her there.

It wasn't even dark yet, so Mustang Sally's dirt parking lot had plenty of room for his crew cab. Inside, a layer of secondhand smoke drifted over their heads and Johnny Cash sang "Hurt" on the jukebox.

A pale-faced girl with long dark hair tied back in a low ponytail and a frayed gray hoodie that read, In My Defense, I Was Left Unsupervised, said, "Well if it isn't our town celebrity and the one and only Jobeth Bravo."

Jo greeted her. "Sabrina, how've you been?"

"Not bad," replied Sabrina as Jobeth leaned across the bar and she and Sabrina shared a quick hug. Sabrina whipped a couple of plastic menus off a metal holder and passed them to Jo. "Seat yourselves. I'll be over in a minute."

Jo led the way to a small table on the edge of the empty dance floor, not far from a doorway that led into a room where shadowy figures bent over pool tables. Balls clicked together. Somebody made a low remark and a woman laughed.

He and Jo sat across from each other at a scarred wood table with a condiment caddy in the middle. Jo grinned at him. "The secondhand smoke is especially authentic, don't you think? You don't get much of that in bars anymore."

He looked around at all the beer signs, the liquor bottles stacked two-deep against the streaky mirror behind the long mahogany bar, the regular customers lined up in a row on their barstools, most of them smoking, hunched over their drinks. "Please don't tell me you come here often…"

She laughed. He loved when she laughed. The sound danced like soft fingers down his spine. Would she shove him away if he grabbed her and laid one on her right now?

Probably.

He kept his hands to himself.

"Nope, I do not come here often," she said. "The

year I turned twenty-one, I was in here a few times with girlfriends in the summertime, exploring the new freedoms of being an adult, you might say. Somehow, the glamor wore off pretty fast."

"So why are we here now?"

She was still leaning in, her face open and eager. Was that a good sign? Damn, he hoped so. "I don't know. I just wanted to mix things up, I guess. To do something different."

"Because you and me, we're in a rut?" he teased.

Before she could come up with an answer, Sabrina appeared with two red plastic water glasses. She set them down. "What'll you two have?"

They ordered burgers and fries, and a couple of beers.

As soon as she left, Jo answered his question. "No, we are not in a rut. How could we be?" She turned her water glass slowly, then picked it up and took a sip. "I started to feel nervous. I was afraid it would be uncomfortable just sitting across from each other in Arlington's, making small talk. At least here, there's the weird roadhouse vibe." She waved her hand in front of her face, disturbing the gray layer of smoke in the air. "Not to mention the ever-present threat of lung cancer. And they have a band that comes on at seven thirty…or maybe eight. I'm not sure. It's usually not a very good band, but so what? We can dance…or not…" Color flooded up under her freckles.

Sabrina reappeared and set down their beers. He waited until the server had moved on, then demanded, "Whatever you were about to say, hit me with it."

"Well, Hunter. It's still awkward. I mean, why are we doing this?"

"Good question," someone said sourly.

Hunter glanced over and saw Nick Collerby standing in the open doorway to the pool room. He had a pool cue in one hand and a beer bottle dangling from the other. His dark blond hair was longer than Hunter remembered. He had on tan slacks, dress boots and an expensive shirt and jacket—everything was a little rumpled, though. He had that look—a man with too many worries out to get good and loose on a Friday night.

"Hello, Jobeth."

"Hey, Nick." Jo tried to sound casual but failed. She looked at least as alarmed as Hunter felt.

And why wouldn't she be surprised to see her ex here? Mustang Sally's was hardly Nick's kind of place—at least not the Nick that Hunter remembered. Nick's dad had sold insurance and made a good living at it. Growing up, Nick lived in a big house in town. He'd played running back on the Medicine Creek High football team. He used to date cheerleaders, but he'd always had his eye on Jo.

Back then, she never would give him the time of day.

A woman in tight jeans with long black hair eased in beside Nick. "Come on, babe," she coaxed. "Your shot."

"Thanks, Aida." He tipped up her chin and gave her a slow kiss. "Be right there…"

Aida made a pouty face but then turned and disappeared into the other room.

Nick sauntered closer. He gave Hunter a nod. "Heard you were back in town. Big star, all that."

Jo sat up straighter. A little wearily, she asked, "What do you want, Nick?"

He gave her a hard stare and a fake smile. "Just thought I'd say hi."

"And you have." She met his eyes squarely. "You take care now."

Nick turned to Hunter again. "I believe I have been dismissed."

Hunter wanted to punch the fool, but it felt wrong to hit a man simply for being a jerk…and maybe also for having been married to Jo. "Good to see you, Nick," he lied.

"Nick, come *on*!" Aida stood in the doorway again.

"In a minute." He threw the words over his shoulder.

"But Nick, it's your—"

"Shut up, Aida!"

Hunter now had a very bad feeling about this visit to Mustang Sally's. He sent a worried glance at Jo. She'd closed her eyes and was shaking her head.

As for Aida, she was coming their way. "Don't you tell me to— Wait." She stepped up beside Nick and braced her fists on her shapely hips. "If it isn't the ex-wife, slumming it at Sally's, her and the big TV star."

Jo was looking right at him now, her eyes wide and worried. Way too quietly, she said, "We should go."

"Good idea." Hunter threw some bills on the table as they rose.

"Wait just a minute." Aida grabbed Jo by the arm. "I got a few things to say to you…"

"Let her go," Hunter and Nick said in unison.

Everybody froze.

And then Aida did let go. She looked at the hand she'd used to grab Jo like there was something disgusting stuck to it. "I don't want to touch her, anyway. She's a heartless cu—"

"Shut your mouth." Nick grabbed Aida and spun her around. "What is the matter with you?"

Aida bared her teeth…and hauled off and slapped Nick. The sound of her palm hitting his cheek echoed like a shot.

About then Hunter noticed that three guys had emerged from the pool room. They had their phones out and were recording the action. The jukebox had started playing "Friends in Low Places." Talk about a little too on-the-nose...

Aida shouted, "I'm doin' it for you, baby! That bitch broke your..." Nick grabbed her by the upper arms. "Ouch! Knock it off!"

Now Nick was shaking her. Hard. "I didn't ask for your help, Aida!"

"You're hurting me!" she screeched.

Hunter believed the woman. Aida's head was whipping back and forth hard enough to cause whiplash, at least. He grabbed Nick by the shoulder.

At the same time, Jobeth cried, "Nick! Let her go..."

Nick did let her go...in order to spin around and punch Hunter in the jaw.

Ears ringing, he went down. Nick jumped on top of him. They rolled around on the sticky floor, Nick trying to land another haymaker, Hunter just trying to get a grip on the other man.

It took him a minute or two, but he managed to get Nick facedown and to yank his arm up behind him, subduing him. Nick's mouth was still working, though. He turned the smoky air blue with the stuff he was spouting.

Still holding the man down, Hunter glanced over and saw Jo sitting on Aida. She had one of Aida's hands locked behind her back in a mirror of Hunter's position on top of Nick.

"All right, kids!" shouted a guy in a deputy's uniform. "That's about enough, now!" He flashed his badge as he strode toward them from the door.

Chapter Five

"It could've been worse," Jo offered sheepishly as she lowered the ice-filled towel away from her swollen cheek.

Hunter was behind the wheel of his truck, driving them back to the ranch. Taking care to make his voice gentle and low, he instructed, "Keep that ice on it."

"I am." Jo pressed the ice back to her cheek.

Aida had punched her a good one before Jo got the upper hand. The server, Sabrina, had offered the improvised ice pack to help keep the swelling down. She'd offered Hunter one, too, but he'd said he was fine.

Wincing, Jo readjusted the towel. "Good thing

those guys were filming it or we'd have been hauled off to County along with Nick and Aida."

Too bad the fight would be all over social media by morning. That could cause all sorts of blow-back for him PR-wise, but Jo was right. Why not look on the bright side? "Good point. We should call ourselves lucky."

Jo frowned as he took a turn onto a dirt road. "Where are we going?"

"You'll see." He topped a rise and below them, gleaming in the moonlight, Crystal Creek was a bright ribbon unfurling, flowing down from the Bighorn Mountains, winding its way over the roll-ing land.

Jo didn't object, so he drove on to the side of the creek and stopped at a flat spot several feet from the water.

When he turned off the engine, the cab got re-ally quiet.

But then Jo let out a long, pained sigh. "I swear," she whispered. "I had no idea this would hap-pen. Never in a million years did I think Nick would be spending his Friday evening at Mustang Sally's. I mean, when we were together he went to a sports bar in Sheridan or that wine bar in Buf-falo when he wanted to get loose and hang out. No dive bars for Nick Collerby. He sells insurance, for heaven's sake."

Hunter leaned toward her, across the console. "Hey."

She gave him a wobbly little smile. "Say you believe me."

He really liked that she cared what he thought, that she didn't want him getting the idea she might be playing games, stirring up trouble with her ex. "I do believe you." He took her hand—the one that wasn't pressing the iced-filled towel to the bruise on her cheek.

She didn't pull away.

Her palm and fingers were calloused, same as he remembered. Calloused and cool. Damn. It felt so good, to touch her. Again. After so damn long. "Sometimes crap happens."

She wrinkled her nose at him. "Ain't that the truth." He rubbed his thumb across the back of her hand. Looking him square in the eye, she said, "I never should have married him. I mean, he was always kind of angry—even when we were kids he would pull mean pranks on me. I told you about that time he tied me to a tree and ran off."

"I remember that story." It occurred to him that he should have punched Nick a few more times when he had the chance. "What a jackass."

"My thoughts exactly—and once, when my mom and I first came to Medicine Creek, before she married my dad, Nick propped a full bucket of ice water over a door and rigged it to the door-knob. My birth father had died not long before and we had only lived in Medicine Creek for a short time then. We were seven, Nick and me, hanging out at his house not far from where my mom and I stayed with Edna when she used to live in town. Nick asked me to go get a box of crayons from his room.

"I was so excited to have a friend in town, you know? I ran in there, all eager to get him what he wanted. I pushed open the door...and a bucket of ice water came right down on my head. Scared me to death. The bucket upended, so the water and ice hit me first. Then the bucket landed upside down with my head inside. It clanged against the top of my skull and since it was covering my face, I couldn't see a thing. I had no idea out what had happened. For a second or two, I thought I'd gone blind. Plus, I was shivering and sopping wet. It was a nightmare to me, pure and simple."

"He always wanted to get your attention."

"Yeah. And always in mean ways. I spent years just trying to avoid him." Her eyes were wide, wounded-looking.

"I know you did."

She pulled her hand away and accused, "I know what you're thinking. And you're right, damn it."

"No, you don't know what I'm thinking, Jo."

"Yes, I do. I married my bully, Hunter. Who does that? I never should have gotten involved with him…" She made a low, angry sound, deep in her throat. "Go ahead. Ask the question."

"You don't really want me to do that."

"Just do it. Just ask it."

"Alright, then, why? Why did you marry him?"

"Because the years were going by, you know? Time was just slipping away and I had no one—and Hunter, Nick did try, at first, after I finished my senior year at UW and came home to stay. He actually seemed easygoing. I really thought he'd changed, that he'd grown up into a good guy. He cut out all the crappy offhand insulting remarks. He was friendly and interested, someone I could like."

Like, he thought. *Not love*. He kept his mouth firmly shut so he wouldn't slip up, say that out loud and get her pissed off at him all over again.

She went on, "He asked me out three times before I finally said I would meet him for dinner at Arlington's."

"Meet him? As in, you drove your own car?"

"Yes."

"Because you still weren't convinced you wouldn't end up with a bucket of ice water dumped on your head."

"Exactly." She pulled the towel away from her swollen cheek and offered it to him.

"Put that back on your cheek, where it belongs."

"He clipped you pretty good on the jaw. We can share."

He tried not to smirk, though it pleased him to no end that she would share her ice pack with him. "I'm okay."

"Come on." She pushed it toward him again. "Take it."

He wanted to hear the rest of the story, so he let her hand him the cold towel. She waited, not saying a word, until he pressed it to the sore spot where Nick's punch had landed. For a few minutes they sat silently staring out the windshield. The creek gleamed under the stars and the dark humps of the mountains rose up, black shadows against the night sky.

He broke the silence. "Go on."

She didn't look at him, kept her gaze aimed straight ahead, on the mountains out there beyond the glass. "I swear, I really thought he'd changed his ways. He was sweet and attentive. It seemed to me that that was who he really was. I thought, well, people do change and maybe it could work out for Nick and me."

"But…?"

"I never planned to tell you all this." She was scowling at him now. "You don't need to hear it."

"I *want* to hear it."

She scoffed. "Fine. After that mess at Sally's, what can I say? You want it, you got it."

He passed her the ice pack.

She pressed it gently to her cheek. "Okay, so I knew he had a thing for me and I was lonely and I wanted a family. He asked me to marry him. I said I would not live anywhere but the Rising Sun. I explained that I can't take care of my horses and work cattle and then go home to my big house on Cedar Street. I said that I have to be there, ready to work when I'm needed. I mean, a dying calf can't just hold on while I drive in from town."

"And what did Nick say to all that?"

"He swore he was good with it, that he would move in with me at the ranch. So we got married and moved into the homesteader's cabin, which has been there since my great-great-grandfather's day. I don't know if you remember it, but it's small and dark and quite a ways from the main house. Nick hated it. I kind of understood that and I wanted more space, too. I'd gotten money from my grandparents back east when I turned twenty-five." She meant Zach's wealthy parents in New York City. "I spent some of that money to build my house."

Hunter reached over the seat for the burgers and fries Sabrina had bagged up to go. At his request, she'd added a couple of cans of Coke.

Jo looked at him, her expression softening. "Can you believe this? A picnic in your pickup..." She laughed. The sound curled around down inside him, warm and right, like a cozy fire on a snowy night.

"Just like old times," he said.

"Exactly…except, you know, much fancier vehicle. And now you're all successful and everything. Killer haircut, by the way."

"I try."

"And divorced, just like me."

He heaved a heavy sigh. "I guess I knew that was coming."

"You have to tell me all about that now, about you and that big-time producer you married."

"Not until you finish telling me about Nick."

"Fine." She pulled the towel away from her cheek and scowled at it. "My improvised ice pack is dripping."

"I noticed that, yeah." He watched a drop of water slide along the side of her neck and thought how there'd been a time when he would have leaned close and licked it right off her.

She was looking at him sideways. "What *are* you thinking?"

"That you're going to have a goose egg on your cheekbone," he lied shamelessly.

She shrugged. "It'll heal. And that's what I get for hanging out at Mustang Sally's." She rolled down her window long enough to throw away the ice and wring out the towel, which she dropped to the floor mat. "Okay, now. Gimme that greasy goodness."

He passed her a burger, a bag of fries, a Coke and half the paper napkins Sabrina had stuffed in with the food.

"Your marriage to Nick," he said. "Please continue."

She stuffed a fry in her mouth and chewed it thoughtfully. "Nick hated living on the ranch, even in the new house. In his defense, he did have a business to run. He'd partnered up with his dad and he needed to be at the office at 8:00 a.m. at least five days a week and sometimes Saturdays. In bad weather, it was always a problem. His dad was pissed off at him. And it didn't take long before Nick was just generally pissed off at me. We argued a lot. And he was drinking too much. I wanted us to go see a therapist. He said no way. He thought we should have a baby."

"And you always wanted kids…"

"Yeah, but not like that. Having a child made no sense to me. We needed to learn to get along with each other first." She was staring out the windshield again, eyes on the mountains. "Then he decided to take an apartment in town so he could stay there when the snow on the roads was a problem." She slid him a glance. "What can I say? It's Medicine Creek. People talk…"

He went ahead and asked, "Nick cheated?"

She nodded. "When I found out, I was done."

"Of course, you were."

"I just couldn't bear to be married to him anymore. I told him I knew he'd been with another woman and I wanted a divorce." She looked down at her half-eaten burger like she couldn't quite figure out what it was doing in her hand…and then went back to staring out the windshield again. "He lost it. Way worse than ever before. Up 'til then, it was just mean words. It had become a pattern for him. He would get tanked up, say awful things to me and then storm out. But when I said I was done with him, he not only yelled and called me all kinds of bad names, he pulled back his arm with his hand in a fist." Hunter saw red as she continued, "I really thought he was going to punch me, you know? And I was trying to decide how I was going to deal with that and how bad it was going to be."

She shifted her gaze back to him. At the sight of his face, she gasped…and then she pinned him with a burning look. "No. Uh-uh. I am serious, Hunter Wayne Bartley. Do not even think about it."

He *was* thinking about it—thinking that he and Nick were going to have a nice, long talk. "Tell me the rest."

"I won't tell you jack, you hear me? I will get

out of this big, shiny crew cab and find my own way home. And I will never speak to you again. I'm not fooling around here. I tell you something in confidence, I expect it to stay that way. You will not fight my battles for me. That is in no way your job. Are we clear on this point?"

He needed to know. "Did he hit you?"

"Answer *my* question."

Now he was the one staring blindly out the windshield. His molars hurt from grinding them together. And, damn it, he got her message loud and clear. If he dealt with Nick, he would never again get so much as the time of day from her. He couldn't stand the thought of that, of there no longer being even a chance they might reconnect someday, somehow.

However, Nick Collerby was just begging for a beatdown and Hunter needed to be the one to take care of that.

He slid a sideways glance at her. She glared at him, chin high, mouth set. Not good.

Tonight, finally, he'd made some real progress with her. He didn't want to go back to how it had been for sixteen endless years.

She was like nobody else. The world just seemed better, everything somehow lit up and shining, now that they were spending a little time together again. He didn't think he could give that up. Not yet. If he handled it right, maybe they could stay in touch when he returned to LA.

No, it wouldn't be what it once was.

But he could talk to her now and then, keep up with her, call himself her friend.

"Answer me, Hunter."

"Yeah, Jo. We're clear. I'll leave him alone."

"Good. Thank you—and no, he didn't hit me. But I knew then that I couldn't back down. I knew that we were done, Nick and me. I knew my marriage was over, that it wouldn't get better, that he would cheat again and he would not go to counselling with me. He would never try to work it out in a reasonable way. I also knew the odds were that someday he *would* actually hit me." She let her head fall back against the headrest. Time ticked by in silence.

Finally, he prompted, "So, then…he left?"

"Yeah, he stormed out and burned rubber driving off, like the overgrown spoiled brat he is. The next day I had all the locks changed. My mom and dad helped me pack up his stuff. Dad drove the truck to town and delivered everything to Nick at that apartment of his. I filed for divorce. In a year, it was over. I was Jobeth Bravo again."

He wanted to touch her, pull her close, hold her. Tell her how sorry he was that he'd let her down, admit out loud his honest regret that he hadn't been there to help her get through it when it all went to hell.

Too bad he had no right to reach for her. And saying how sorry he was?

Too little, too late.

She wrapped what was left of her burger in its greasy wrapper again. "I've lost my appetite."

"Jo…"

Drawing herself up straight in her seat, she faced him eye-to-eye. "Take me home, Hunter. This evening is over."

He didn't see her all weekend.

Okay, it was only two days. But it felt like a lifetime. He hung around the ranch, hoping for a chance to talk with her a little, to get past what she'd told him Friday night at Crystal Creek.

No luck, though. He didn't so much as catch a glimpse of her that weekend and he was at the ranch the whole time. Both Saturday and Sunday, he had a construction crew at the bunkhouse, getting things up to speed there.

They'd kind of let the bunkhouse lag behind the other projects. It was the most accessible job, after all—the only job where the facility wouldn't be in use during the project. That made everything a lot easier.

And it turned out to be good for him, to focus

on work, get his mind off his fear that he'd blown it with Jo.

The bunkhouse was a ramshackle, tumbledown barnlike structure and Zach had been using it for storage. Hands on the Rising Sun didn't need it. They all brought trailers to live in.

But when Hunter approached Zach months ago, Jo's dad had said he'd always wanted a real bunkhouse on the ranch, one with a nice central living area and simple, comfortable bedrooms, each with its own small bath. Zach said if the hands didn't want to use it, relatives and friends could stay there when they visited.

Zach Bravo had money to burn. Jobeth had once confided in Hunter that her dad's family in New York had plenty of money and Zach had invested his inheritance wisely. Yes, he kept the Rising Sun in the black, but he lived the ranching life because he loved it, same as his adopted daughter, who was nowhere to be seen on Monday, either.

That day, they filmed bunkhouse scenes for the show. The construction workers, all local guys, provided background action while he conferred with Zach about what progress they'd made and the new issues that would need tackling.

Hunter had dinner that night at the main house. Once again, Jo failed to join them.

Later, he took a walk around the yard to stretch

his legs a little…or so he told Tess as he went out the door. It was only an excuse to find out if Jo was home yet. Tess knew it, too. She gave him that sly little smile of hers, the one that said she was on to him.

So what? He walked the circular driveway around the central open area presided over by a handsome maple tree. The maple hadn't been there back when he left town. A big Russian olive tree had filled the space then.

Overhead, the sky showed layers of purple and orange as night came on and light shone from the windows and the glass of the front door at Jo's house. He stopped at the foot of her walk and debated marching up the steps and knocking.

Debating was all he did. As he stood there, the wind came up and it started to rain—big drops that made pinging sounds as they hit the ground. Drenched to the skin in a few short minutes, he headed back to the main house.

Jo might be MIA, but not her big sister.

Tuesday morning at seven, when Hunter arrived at Crystal Creek Lodge for a full day of taping, Starr was already there. In a bright red maternity dress that clung to the bold jut of her enormous belly, Jo's big sister sat in a folding chair. She had her open laptop balanced on what was left of her lap. Her fingers flew over the keys as she tapped out the third installment of her *Hunter Comes Home* series of editorials for the *Clarion*.

She glanced up at him with a giant, glowing smile, typed another furious torrent of words and then paused. "Hunter, I have to say it. You just might be my favorite person in the whole world right now." She looked at him from under her impossibly long, thick black eyelashes. "Please don't tell Beau."

What was she getting at? He wasn't sure he wanted to know.

As he tried to decide how to respond, she laughed. "You should see your face."

"Not sure what you're up to, that's all."

"It's simple. You are pure gold in this town. The past two weeks, since I started my series about the show, everybody wants a copy of the *Medicine Creek Clarion*. Our online subscriptions have doubled. Our ad buys are up. I thank you and the *Clarion* thanks you."

By then, he was smiling, too. "Glad to hear it."

Mel called, "Hunter! I need a minute…"

"On my way…"

Starr gave him a nod and then started pounding the laptop keys again.

Hunter joined Mel and David. The two sat side by side in matching director's chairs with their names on the back. His own chair sat empty on the far side of David. Neither of them got up and he didn't sit down.

Mel gave him her sharklike grin. "Noticed you had an exciting Friday night at an interesting place called Mustang Sally's." The incident with Nick and Aida had gotten way too much social-media attention over the weekend. "Tell all about that special girl, Hunter?"

"Aida? Never met her before. Didn't get her last name."

"Please. Jobeth Bravo. Zach's daughter—Starr's sister."

"Jobeth and I went to school together."

"Ugh. I already know that. You are not the least forthcoming…and can we get your old school chum on tape?"

"I thought we settled this before."

Mel scoffed, "You thought wrong."

"The answer is no."

"Sometimes you are a real pain in my ass," she muttered.

David waved a hand. "Moving on. Did Starr mention the interview?"

Hunter's puzzled expression must have said it all because Mel immediately asked, "So Starr hasn't told you, then?"

He looked from Mel to the director and back to Mel again. "Just fill me in. What's going on?"

David explained, "Starr will interview you on tape this afternoon—she'll use the interview as a transcript for her column this week, and we'll put the best moments from the tape on the show."

It was beginning to look like one of those days. "We're already scheduled to shoot all day. Can't we fit this interview in some other time?"

Mel clucked her tongue and chided, "Oh, Hunter." Rising from her chair, she took him by the shoulders and turned him around so he was facing Starr. "Look at her," Mel whispered in his ear. "Fans of *Rebuilt by Bartley* are going to love her and she is about to pop. We are going to get her on tape before she has that baby. Then later, we'll talk her into some family shots—her and the devoted hubby, the adorable newborn and the rest of the kids. She has other kids, right?"

Several days ago, Tess had bragged to him that Starr's oldest, Elizabeth, had earned a full ride to UCLA. Second-born Sawyer was still in high school. "She has a daughter in college and a son at Medicine Creek High."

"A daughter in college?" Mel demanded, "How old *is* she?"

"Early forties."

"Damn. She looks good. But then, forty is the new twenty-five, right? And as for the older kids, we'll get them on tape, too. It's going to be fabulous."

And he would most likely have no time for stalking Jobeth this evening, that was for certain. "What you're telling me is that tonight I'll be eating dinner off the craft-services table."

"Hunter…" Mel clucked her tongue some more. "Won't we all?"

Leonard Stevely, owner and manager of the Crystal Creek Lodge and Cabins, was shy. The cameras intimidated him. Taping that day went long.

Starr had disappeared around lunchtime. Hunter never got around to asking Mel if the interview had been officially postponed. He hoped so, but he was kind of busy trying to put Leonard at ease and fielding calls from the construction crews at the other locations. They had a minor flood at the chamber of commerce, where the plumbing diagrams hadn't matched up to the pipes in the walls of the small kitchen there.

At five thirty, David called a halt for the day. Hunter had dared to hope he might escape.

But then Starr sailed back in.

Elinor Cristal, their one-woman hair and makeup crew, fussed over Jo's sister for ten minutes or so. When Starr's lips were cherry-red and her hair had been brushed out and fell just so on her shoulders, Hunter sat down with her right there in the rustic lobby of the lodge. Starr took one of the club chairs. Hunter got the ancient corduroy sofa.

Starr opened the interview with questions about Hunter's days growing up in Medicine Creek. She kept it light, fun and not too personal. Just the basics—that he'd learned his trade from his dad and headed off for LA the summer after his senior year. He was grateful that she didn't bring Jo into it, though he'd been pretty sure she wouldn't. Jobeth would not have wanted that, and Starr and Jo always had each other's backs.

Starr asked, "Tell me, Hunter. Did you learn how to surf out there in Los Angeles?"

They shared a secret smile. Jo must have told her that he used to claim he would buy a surfboard first thing, as soon as he got to LA. And he'd done it, too. He'd found a cheap board at a surf shop in Santa Monica and rented a studio apartment in Pacoima, where the crime rate was pretty high, but housing came relatively cheap. Right away, he started getting work as a handyman.

"Yes, I did learn to surf," he said. "I'm no Kelly Slater, but I do manage to, uh, catch a wave now and then."

"Well, I can just picture you in board shorts and…" Starr never finished that sentence. Her face had paled. "Oh," she said. "Oh! This is just…oh!"

Wrapping her arms around her belly, she let out a long, pained moan.

He jumped up. "Starr?"

"Hunter, I think we're going to have to finish this interview later..."

"Sure. Of course. What can I do?"

"My water just broke. Get me to the hospital. Please."

Chapter Six

Things got a little chaotic after that. David kept the cameras going longer than he should have and that pissed Hunter off. A woman in labor ought to be given some damn privacy and she sure as hell ought to be more important than juicy footage for a home-improvement show.

"Where's your truck?" Starr demanded.

"Right outside the door."

"Perfect." She pushed herself to her feet with effort. And then she glanced down at the puddle where she'd been sitting. "What a mess."

"Hey," he said. "Don't even think twice about that. Leonard's replacing all the furnishings in here."

"I'm very glad to hear that—grab my laptop and my bag?"

"Got 'em."

"Thank you, Hunter."

By then, David and Mel had finally rearranged their priorities. They came bustling over, followed by Rudy Bales, the production coordinator. All of them were now talking at once in a flood of over-the-top sympathy and concern.

Starr turned to him again and muttered, "Let's make a break for it."

"You got it." He took her arm. She leaned on him as they rounded the sofa table and approached the double doors leading out to the gravel parking lot.

"What can we do? Who can we call?" Mel demanded as Hunter backed one of the doors open to clear the way for Starr.

"We're good," Hunter said.

Starr managed a wave. "I'll call my husband on the way. No worries. We're off to Memorial!"

"Memorial what?" Rudy demanded.

"Hospital! In Sheridan!" Starr fired the words over her shoulder as Hunter herded her toward the crew cab.

He beeped the locks, helped her up into the seat and raced around to the driver's side. "Where's your phone?" he asked as he climbed up behind the wheel.

"It's in my bag." She reached for it.

He handed it over and put the laptop on the back seat.

"Oh, no!" she cried.

He glanced at her again, alarmed. "What is it?" She was looking down at her lap. "Starr, what can I do?"

"I'm so sorry," she moaned. "I'm leaking all over this pretty leather seat."

"Don't worry about it," he advised as he started the engine. "The production company pays for insurance. We're fully covered, I promise." He added sheepishly, "And I know the last thing you need is a seat belt around your belly right now, but do you think you could stand to buckle up?"

She groaned some more, but she did it.

"You're a trooper, Starr."

"You bet I am. Get me out of here!"

He brought up the map, told Google where he wanted to go and off they went.

During the twenty-minute drive, Starr made several calls. When he pulled up at the hospital's main entrance, there was a guy in scrubs waiting for her with a wheelchair. Hunter jumped out to help, but the guy had it handled.

"I'll park and then bring in your laptop," he offered.

"Thank you," she said as the orderly wheeled her chair around and headed for the entrance.

When Hunter got to the front desk a few minutes later, the receptionist pointed the way to Women's Health, Labor and Delivery. He took a seat in the waiting area there, figuring he would give Starr's laptop to whichever family member showed up first and then head back to Medicine Creek.

Didn't quite work out that way.

Tess and Edna arrived first. Tess gave him a grateful smile. "Thank you, Hunter, for looking after our girl."

"Of course."

"Is Beau with her?"

"I don't think he's here yet."

Tess patted Edna's arm. "I'll just get them to take me to Starr. She needs someone with her, at least until Beau arrives."

"Yes. You go on, now…" Edna grabbed her in a hug and then Tess bustled off toward the nurses' station.

As for Edna, she plopped down next to him and started asking questions. She'd already heard that Starr's water had broken in the middle of their interview. Now, she wanted the full story of how he'd rescued Starr from the TV people and rushed her to Memorial.

He'd just finished filling her in when Beau and Sawyer showed up. A nurse came right away and led Beau off to be with Starr. Sixteen-year-old

Sawyer, who had the same sandy hair and lean, strong build as his dad, said a polite hello to Edna, greeted Hunter and then sprawled in a chair, pulled out his phone and started playing a video game.

Leaning close, Edna whispered, "Lizzie's still down in Los Angeles until June." Lizzie was Starr and Beau's firstborn.

He nodded. "She's at UCLA—I remember."

Edna patted his hand and began rambling on about how fast all the kids were growing up. "My grandbabies have babies now. Tyler Ross is twenty-eight." Ty was the older son of Zach's cousin Cash and Edna's daughter, Abby. "Do you believe that?" She went right on before he could answer. "Ty married Nicole Haralson right out of high school. Sadly, the marriage didn't last. Ty and Nicole divorced a few years back, but they did give me two gorgeous great-grandbabies, Emily and Drew."

"Ah," he said.

Apparently *ah* was enough. She told him about Ty's younger brother, Joshua, and then about how much she still missed her own husband, who had died the same year Ty was born.

"But look at me, rambling on." She patted his hand again. "And I can't say it enough. We are just so grateful that you were there to look after Starr when she needed you."

"Happy to help," he said, and was just about to

add how he really should be on his way when Tess returned from the delivery room.

Jo's mom launched into an update on Starr's condition. "It's all going well," she said and then continued with some other stuff about dilation and effacement and how labor was progressing quickly, but not to worry. All the vital signs were strong and Starr was holding up just fine.

"Oh, and Hunter," Tess added. "I'll take that laptop. She wants it." He handed it over. "You know how she is." Tess shook her head. "Only Starr would think she had to keep working on her newspaper in the middle of having her baby."

Edna said, "You really do have to tell her to focus on the baby right now."

Tess gave a low laugh. "And how much good do you think my telling her that is going to do?"

Edna's sigh was long and weary. "I know, I know."

"I'm humoring her."

"Fair enough." The two women nodded at each other, apparently in perfect understanding, as Sawyer went right on playing his game.

Tess said, "I'll just go on back to her." She held up the laptop. "Hunter, thank you again."

Tess had just vanished through the doors into the labor and delivery rooms when Jobeth and Zach arrived. They had on work shirts and dusty jeans. Jo's hair was tied in a low ponytail, silky strands escaping, like the wind had teased them free. She and her dad must have been out working into the evening, moving stock or fixing fences. Only the faintest bruise remained where Aida had punched her.

When she spotted him sitting there next to Edna, her eyes got big and wary. She bit the inside of her cheek. But then she slid him a tiny, nervous smile.

No way was he going anywhere now.

"How's Starr doing?" Zach asked.

Edna launched into a repeat of what Tess had just told them.

When she finished, Zach turned to Hunter. "I understand we have you to thank for getting her to the hospital in time. I appreciate that."

Edna asked Zach, "Did you and Jobeth get something to eat before you left?"

"We didn't, but we'll live, don't worry. I want to be right here when there's news."

Jo said, "How about I go get us something from the cafeteria?"

Hunter saw his chance and grabbed it. "I didn't eat, either. I'll come with you."

"You really don't have to—"

"But I want to. Edna, what can we bring you?" He whipped out his phone and brought up the notes app.

"Lovely idea, dear. A sandwich, any kind, would

be so nice. And hot tea would be wonderful—just regular tea, whatever they have is perfect."

"We'll get that." He typed in her order.

Zach said, "A sandwich and a coffee sounds good. And you two don't have to rush back just to sit here in the waiting room and eat off your laps. Take your time."

Hunter slid a glance at Jo and found her looking sideways back at him. "Alright, then," he said, as he typed in Zach's order.

Sawyer glanced up from his phone. "I'll take a burger, fries and a Dr Pepper, thanks."

Jo started walking. Hunter fell in beside her.

In the cafeteria, they both decided on the meat loaf and claimed an empty table not far from the serving line.

"Where's Paisley?" he asked as he spread his paper napkin on his lap.

"Mom took her to Abby's." Edna's daughter and her husband, Cash, lived in town. "I'll pick her up on the way home."

He shoveled in a bite of meat loaf, gulped down some milk and asked, "So how've you been since Friday night?"

She sent him a look, a testy one, but with a glint of humor that gave him way more hope than he probably should let himself feel. "I suppose you're aware that those fools who had their phones out put it on Facebook."

"I saw that."

"Instagram, too, or so I heard. Probably Tik-Tok and YouTube and every other random social-media outlet there is." She ate some mashed potatoes. "I'm not even on most of them. But everyone I talk to is only too happy to give me a heads-up. Luckily, I spend all day with cattle and horses, and they never say a word about my bad judgment Friday night." She shrugged. "I'm telling myself it could be worse."

Jo was a very private person. He'd kind of assumed she would be upset when she saw the clips.

He said, "You seem to be taking it pretty well."

"Meh. Fools will be fools, right?"

That made him smile. "Absolutely."

"And Hunter…"

"Yeah?"

"I, um, guess I kind of overreacted—when I thought you might go after Nick."

He looked in those eyes of hers and never wanted to look away. "It's alright."

"No, it's not. I don't know why I told you all that, about Nick and me, about how it ended. I shouldn't have said—"

"Stop."

She sat back in her chair. "What?"

"I'm glad that you told me. And I should have been more respectful. Nick did you wrong and you handled it just right. End of story."

Her cheeks had gone sweetly pink. "Well. I'm glad to hear you say that." She raised her glass of milk. He grabbed his and they tapped them together. "Here's to you, Hunter. Thank you for being there for my sister today."

They finished the meal, bought the food and drinks her family had asked for and carried it all back to the waiting room.

Tess came out of the delivery room just as they got there. She was beaming.

Zach jumped up. "Is she…?"

"Mother and daughter are doing fine," Tess announced.

Zach grabbed her and kissed her. When he lifted his head, she said, "Your granddaughter, Cara Grace, is seven pounds, three ounces and absolutely beautiful. Her Apgar score is nine and that is excellent."

"When can we see her?" asked Edna.

A half an hour later, Starr and Cara Grace had been moved out of the birthing suite and into a maternity room. Beau was with them. One at a time, starting with Zach, the rest of them got to meet the new baby.

Hunter probably would have passed when his turn came, but Tess and Edna insisted. He went in and Starr was lying there looking flushed, sweaty and exhausted. Both she and Beau encouraged him to hold Cara. He took the tiny, blanket-wrapped baby into his arms. She yawned and sighed, and never once opened her eyes.

When he got back to the waiting room, it was after ten. Everyone was talking about heading home for the night as he shamelessly tried to think of a way to get another moment or two with Jo.

He slid her a glance.

And found she was watching him, those aquamarine eyes of hers kind of misty. His heart went wild, like it was trying to beat its way out of his chest to get to her.

She patted the empty seat beside her.

Jobeth had to hold back a ridiculous giggle at the look on Hunter's face when she signaled him over.

Really, he was such a good guy. She wouldn't have fallen hopelessly and completely in love with him all those years ago if he hadn't been.

But still, she felt at a loss around him—weak. Vulnerable. Scared she would get her heart shattered all over again. The pain when he'd left her all those years ago had been unbearable.

She didn't want to suffer like that again. Sometimes she couldn't help thinking she would be better off to just leave all that love stuff alone.

Except, well...

She still had those feelings whenever she got

near him—the butterflies in the belly, the heat, the yearning that made it hard to breathe.

How was she supposed to just pretend that he didn't affect her?

Hunter Bartley made her feel so acutely alive. She'd spent weeks doing her level best to avoid him. But keeping him at bay hadn't made her stop wanting him.

Slowly, her attitude toward the situation had shifted.

More and more now, she found herself thinking, so what if it wouldn't last forever? She was thirty-four years old and very well aware that life didn't dish up all those passionate, heart-pounding feelings every day of the week.

Maybe, instead of trying to get away from him, she needed to grab on tight and enjoy the ride.

"Did you get to hold Cara?" she whispered when he sat down beside her.

"I did. She's very small. And gorgeous."

"Isn't she, though? Starr told me you hooked her up with your producer and director."

"Nah. Starr's a force, Jo. She made that happen all by herself."

"You opened the door for her. And she's so grateful. She bought the *Clarion* from Jerry Espinoza five years ago." Jerry had been the owner and editor of the paper for decades. "At least it didn't cost her much. Newspapers are closing up shop all over the country, after all. But Starr believes in that paper. She loves it almost as much as she loves Beau and their kids. She'll do just about anything to make a go of it. And *Hunter Comes Home* is helping her with that."

"I'm glad—truth is, everybody's happy about Starr and her newspaper. My director and producer are all over her."

"Um. In a good way, I hope."

"Mostly. They can be obsessive."

"No problem. Starr can handle that."

"Jo?" her dad asked as he pulled his canvas jacket off the back of his chair. "You want to take my truck? I can ride home with Tess and Edna."

Hunter leaned closer. "Let me take you."

She met his eyes and felt herself sinking happily into them. "I have to stop in town to pick up Paisley at Abby's."

"Then we'll stop at Abby's first."

She should probably turn him down.

But forget that. Life didn't always have to be about doing what she *should* do. "Thanks, Dad. Hunter will take me. I'll just grab the car seat from your truck before you go…"

A light was on in the front room when Hunter pulled up in front of Abby's big house in town.

"Be right back." Jo jumped out before he could say a word in reply.

He watched her run up the walk and disappear inside. She reemerged a few moments later with her baby on one shoulder and a diaper bag on the other. The baby let out a few fussy noises as Jo put her in her seat in back, but quickly quieted.

Jo jumped in beside him, plunking down on the lap blanket he'd thrown on the seat to cover the damp spot Starr had been so worried about. They rode to the ranch in silence, now and then glancing across the console at each other, making eye contact, sharing smiles.

At her house, he jumped out of the truck before she could tell him not to. He carried the car seat inside and waited in the main room while she put Paisley to bed.

DC came slinking out from under a chair and strolled on over to rub against his legs. Hunter scooped him up and scratched him under the collar. "You're getting pretty hefty there, big boy."

"Reow," DC replied, and squirmed to get down.

"Sorry." Hunter set down the cat. "No offense intended."

DC strutted off without a backward glance as Jo emerged from the baby's room. "So," she said and folded her arms across her middle, the pose as uncomfortable as the expression on her face. "What now?"

"I could go for a nice hot decaf."

"I can do that." She led him to the kitchen area and gestured at the central table. He sat down.

The silence between them continued as she made the coffee. He really didn't mind the quiet, but she kept glancing over her shoulder at him. Either she was leading up to some difficult question, or she really wished he would just go, leave her alone, stop chasing after her when she had no intention of being caught.

Finally, she set a full mug in front of him and took the chair next to him at the head of the table. Her knee brushed his when she sat down.

The contact soothed him and his apprehensions eased a little. Her hand was right there, resting on the tabletop, inches away.

He put his hand over it and felt her stiffen slightly in reaction. "Breathe," he suggested in a teasing tone as he eased his thumb and fingers beneath her palm, curling his hand around hers, holding on.

She looked directly at him then, her eyes wide open, full of things he really hoped she would actually say. "It was awful when you left me to move to LA. I thought I would never get over you."

"I've missed you, too," he whispered. "Every day. For sixteen years."

Her smile was slow and very sad. "Then why didn't you just come back?"

"I am back."

"Took you long enough." She shook her head. "Just kidding…but not."

"Yeah. I get that."

"Hunter, I did understand why you had to go. At the same time, I wanted you to love *me* more than you needed to get away."

"I know."

She curled her fingers around his. Now they were both holding on. He focused on how good that felt as she said, "And I'm thinking you felt pretty much the same way I did, that I didn't love you enough to go with you, that I chose home and my family and the Rising Sun over you."

"Jo, we were eighteen. Give us a break, why don't you?"

They both snickered at that and she said, "Isn't it terrific that we're so much more mature now?"

"It is, yeah." He said it without much enthusiasm.

"And you're stalling." She pinned him with a challenging glare. "It's your turn. I want you to tell me about your ex-wife, Lauren Maris, about why you got married and why you're not married anymore."

"Do we really have to…?"

"Yes. We do. We really do."

"Most of that story is public knowledge. You can pretty much just google it."

"I did." She eased her hand free of his. He let

go reluctantly. They both sipped coffee. Finally, she grumbled, "And now you probably think I've been stalking you..."

"Hey, a man can hope."

"Well, I'll have you know I haven't."

"O-kay..."

"Or at least, I didn't for the longest time." She picked up her coffee again and sipped from it. "Though I admit, I wanted to. But I never gave in to the urge until recently, not long after I lied to my dad and said I had no problem with your staying here at the ranch while you're in town."

It was one of those moments. He really wanted to grab her and kiss her, to crush her soft mouth with his again, to feel her body pressed to his. His skin felt electrified, the air in the room crackling with want. "So then what *do* you know about Lauren and me?"

"Well, I know that she's a producer with a couple of successful home-remodeling shows. I read that she hired you as a handyman and you two hit it off, that she thought you had the right combination of construction skills, good looks and personality to be a home-improvement star, so she put you in one of her shows."

"That's true. I liked her. She liked me. We started dating. We got married." He waited for her to ask him if he'd been in love with Lauren. And then he couldn't decide whether to be relieved or disappointed that she didn't. "Lauren is smart and funny and tough. She's also ambitious. Everything is about work with her. She was always pushing. She wants her own home-improvement show empire and she wanted me to want that, too."

"But you didn't?"

"Not the way she wanted it. She wanted us to build that empire of hers together. And I..." He'd wanted to feel what he'd felt with the woman sitting next to him now. But he never had. "The way I saw it, Lauren and I had no life. For her, it was all about our careers. I wanted more. I wanted to head for the beach every once in a while, to go places for the fun of it, places where there was zero opportunity for networking. And I was starting to admit to myself that someday I really did want kids."

"But she was all about work and she didn't want kids?"

"That's it. And it's not that she'd lied to me. She hadn't. She'd been upfront from the first. Work was her happy place. And we'd agreed before we got married that neither of us wanted children. Basically, we got married first and then had to face the fact that we wanted different things."

The story of his marriage made Jo sad. "I'm sorry, Hunter."

"Don't be. Lauren and I are on good terms now. We really are better off as friends."

She wasn't sure what to say to that. From the way he'd told the story, it seemed pretty clear that he'd never truly loved his ex-wife. And that just wasn't right.

But who was she to judge? Look at her and Nick. She'd married Nick out of loneliness, pure and simple.

Hunter watched her now through hooded eyes. "Sometimes I do regret it—leaving you."

She confessed, "I know the feeling. I will always regret losing you."

He took her hand again. She let him. It felt so good to have his fingers woven with hers. In a strange way, his touch settled the wild yearning he stirred in her. "Too bad the ending of our story is always the same," he said. "You wouldn't go. And I couldn't stay."

She put her other hand over his, clasping it between both of hers. "And knowing you now, seeing how far you've come, how much you've accomplished… Hunter, I get it now. I can accept it now. You needed to go, same as I needed to stay right here." Despite the loneliness that hollowed her out sometimes at night when her little girl was sleeping and she was awake in the dark, all alone, she couldn't completely regret staying right here on the land she loved.

His eyes saw too much. "What is it? What's wrong?"

She didn't know how to answer him. The truth was too painful, yet a lie seemed so cowardly.

"Jo…" He pulled his hand from her grip, but only in order to frame her face in his big, warm palms.

Heaven. Just to be here with him when she'd long ago given up any hope of such a thing. To feel his hands against her cheeks when she'd resigned herself to the fact that he would never touch her again.

"Jo…"

She watched his eyes, a velvet, shining darkness flecked with gold, as he leaned even closer. She just kept staring into him, steadily holding his gaze right up until the thrilling, perfect moment when his lips touched hers.

Chapter Seven

"Good..." She breathed the word against his parted lips.

He gave it back to her. "So good..."

He smelled the same as she remembered, like a warm night in the woods, like pine trees and earth and somehow burnt sugar, too.

There was no one else like him. Never in her whole life.

She gasped as his tongue slipped between her welcoming lips. Her body burned. The need rose within her, to push her chair back, capture one of the strong hands that cradled her face and then drag him to her bedroom...

With a moan, she broke the delicious, perfect kiss.

Facts had to be faced. They were headed just

one place when it came right down to it—no, two places really.

Her bed.

For a while.

Her bed and then nowhere.

Because in the end he would leave again.

And tonight, all she could think about that was...*so be it*. His ultimate departure couldn't keep her from falling into bed with him. Not in the long run.

His eyes were on her, knowing her. He saw that she wasn't ready to give in to the inevitable. Not yet. Softly, he whispered, "I'd better go."

She wanted to stop him. But she didn't.

She walked him out to the porch and watched him drive the short distance to the main house. He parked the car in the cleared space next to the house and ran up the steps, pausing at the door, turning to give her a wave.

She waved back. A moment later, he disappeared inside.

"Shut the door," Starr commanded. "Quick! And lock it."

After smiling apologetically at sweet old Daniel Hart, who was looking at her hopefully from a few feet down the hall, Jobeth shifted Paisley to her left arm, then shut and locked the door to baby Cara's room.

Starr, in a rocker by the window, glanced up from the newborn nursing at her breast. "What's with the sad face?"

"I just shut the door on Daniel." Daniel was like a father to Beau and a grandad to Lizzie and Sawyer...and no doubt to baby Cara now, too. "I feel just plain mean."

"Ack!" Paisley squirmed to be let down. "Go-dah!" It was a command.

Jobeth eased the diaper bag off her shoulder and put it by the door. Then she set her daughter on the floor. Paisley got right up on her hands and knees and speed-crawled to Cara's crib, where she pulled herself upright.

"Everybody's hovering," Starr grumbled. She looked down at Cara and sighed as a tender smile curved her lips. "Yes, you are beautiful," she said to the baby. She smoothed Cara's dark, wispy hair before glaring at Jo again. "I may need you to break me out of here."

"What? Wait. You had a baby two days ago. You need to take it easy."

"I need to get into town and check on things at the *Clarion*."

"No, you don't." The *Clarion*'s former editor, Jerry Espinoza, had agreed to come out of retirement and run things for as long as Starr needed him. "Starr. The paper came out this morning, as always. I got my copy. It looks great. Jerry still knows what he's doing."

"I saw. He even put the whole story of Cara's birth in 'Over the Back Fence.'" The weekly what's-new-in-the-neighborhood column had run in the *Clarion* for as long as Jobeth could remember. Originally, it had been written by a lovely old lady named Mabel Ruby. Mabel still had the by-line and most likely always would, though she'd passed away more than a decade before. Starr herself had been writing the column since she first went to work for Jerry twenty years ago.

"Come on, now," Jo coaxed. "You have to admit it. The column *was* kind of hilarious—I mean, with you going into labor in the middle of that interview with Hunter. Jerry must have talked to everyone who was anywhere near the Crystal Creek Lodge when it happened."

"You bet he did," Starr remarked darkly. "Jerry's the best. It's a great story."

"So then what are you pissed off about?"

"I guess mostly just the loss of my dignity. Did you happen to notice that the column includes a description of Hunter herding me out to his pickup while amniotic fluid drips down my legs?"

"As you always say, it's the details that make the story."

"We both know that Mabel Ruby would never have used the words *amniotic fluid* in her column."

"Well, everybody knows that Mabel doesn't write that column anymore, so who cares?"

"*I* care." Starr sent her another sour glance and groused, "I just don't like sitting around, you know? And suddenly everybody wants to wait on me. You know I couldn't live without Beau. But does the man *have* to hover? This morning Sawyer cooked me breakfast and then served it to me. Sawyer has never in his life waited on anyone, not that I know about, not until today. It's bizarre."

"They love you."

"I love them, too. But they need to step back and let me breathe."

Jo caught sight of Paisley across the room. "Whoa…" Jumping up and darting over there, she grabbed the little adventurer before she could put out an eye on the corner of the changing table.

Paisley did not approve. "Naw, Maw-maw!" She squirmed in Jo's hold and made grabby hands toward the changing table.

Jo sent a sheepish glance at Starr. "I think she wants that plush elephant." The toy was sitting on the shelf above the table, along with piles of onesies, diapers and other baby paraphernalia.

"Give it to her quick before Cara starts wailing, too."

Jo grabbed the stuffy and Paisley grabbed it from her. "Dow, Maw!"

"Yes, ma'am." Jo set her on the floor, where she plunked to her butt. Hugging the toy hard enough to strangle it, she cooed out a long chain of syllables that almost sounded like real words.

"It's really amazing that she's talking already," Starr marveled as she carefully settled the newborn at her other breast.

"Giving orders in her own private language already is more like it."

"Good luck keeping up with her."

"Thanks. I'll need it." Jo got down on the floor next to Paisley, who promptly crawled into her lap. Jo cuddled her daughter while Paisley fussed over the stuffed elephant and then started chewing on its trunk. "Hey, now…" She started to take the toy away.

Paisley clutched it tighter. "Naw, Maw-maw!"

Starr laughed. "It's fine. I bought that elephant myself. Clearly it was meant to be a gift from me to my favorite niece." She sighed. "And would you look at the two of us? Both of us with babies at the same time. Who knew?"

"I love it."

"Me, too. So…?" Starr said the word on a rising inflection.

"*So* what?"

"I heard about your dustup Friday night at Mustang Sally's."

"Yeah. I think everybody's heard about that by now—not to mention, seen the video. What a disaster. Never in a thousand years did I imagine that we'd run into Nick there."

"I checked with my sources…"

"And?"

Starr stroked the back of a finger along Cara's plump cheek. "Nick posted bail right away—for both him and a woman named Aida Ketchum, who works as a maid at Piney Woods Inn and Suites."

"Good to know." Jo kissed her daughter on the top of her curly head. "I mean, Nick has anger issues. He never could control that temper of his. As for Aida, let's just say that on Friday night, Nick laid the fire and she lit the match. But still, I'm glad to hear neither of them had to spend the night in jail."

"You don't look all that glad."

"Yeah. We shouldn't even have been there. Hunter was taking me to Arlington's. I'm the one who suggested Sally's. I don't know why. I couldn't believe I was going out to dinner with him and I felt driven to screw everything up, I guess. And I did screw it up, royally."

"Hey."

"Hmm?"

"You're staring into space, Jo. Are you sure you're okay?"

"Yep." Jo blinked and focused on her sister, who had the tiny new baby on her shoulder now. A giant burp escaped Cara.

The sisters grinned at each other.

"Things with Hunter...?" Starr prompted.

"Oh, Starr. It's like he's been gone forever. At the same time, it's like he never left me."

Starr rocked her baby. "I knew it. It's not over between the two of you, is it?"

Paisley climbed from Jobeth's lap and flopped to her back on the floor. Hugging the stuffed elephant, she sucked her thumb and stared contentedly up at the ceiling.

Jo grumbled, "It's never going to go anywhere between Hunter and me."

"Ri-i-i-ight."

"He drove me home from the hospital night before last. We talked. It was good, just talking. It felt a little like we were making peace, letting go of what happened sixteen years ago so we could both move on, you know?"

"Move on with your separate lives you mean—him in LA and you here at home?"

"How else is it going to go? He has his life and I have mine. We're literally a thousand miles apart. It can never go anywhere."

"That's the second time you've said that in the

past minute and a half. Who, exactly, are you trying to convince?"

Jo puffed out her cheeks with a hard breath. "Well, not you. That's for sure."

"Good. As you've noticed, I'm not buying. I'll tell you what *I* think…"

"Of course, you will."

"Maybe it's not workable for the two of you long-term. But not every relationship has to be forever."

"I know that. I've been thinking that, too."

"I'm glad to hear you admit it. Because frankly, my take on the situation is that if Hunter Bartley wants to scoop you up and carry you off to bed…"

Jobeth groaned and covered her face with her hands.

"Look at me," Starr commanded. Jo dropped her hands. "Tell me the truth."

"Fine. It's no longer about whether it will happen or not. It's going to happen, I know it and he knows it. The only question now is how bad will it be when he leaves?"

That night seemed as good a night as any to share dinner with the family at the main house, Jobeth decided. She hadn't made the effort since last week—the night Hunter had failed to show until she was back at her house. He might not make it for dinner tonight, either.

Didn't matter, she decided. The important thing was spending a little time with the folks and her brother…and if Hunter was there, well, that would be great, too.

She and Paisley went to the main house at five thirty. Her mom gave her a hug, took the baby and asked her to set the table. According to Edna, before Hunter left that morning, he'd said he would be back for the meal, so Jo set a place for him. But when they sat down to fried chicken, mashed potatoes and her mom's yummy squash casserole, Hunter had not arrived.

They were passing the food around when Jo heard the front door open. Winston, stretched out on the floor not far from her dad's chair, lifted his head and let out a whine.

"Settle," her dad commanded the dog.

"That'll be Hunter," said her mom.

He must have stopped off to wash his hands in the powder room off the entry, because a few minutes crawled by before he appeared in the arch to the formal living room. His gaze found her and lingered for a fraction of a second before he said to her mom, "Sorry I'm late. Taping went long."

Tess gave him her warm smile. "I knew you wouldn't want to miss my fried chicken."

"It's the best." Her dad gave the food his seal of

approval. "And these mashed potatoes will make all your troubles fade clean away."

After they'd loaded up their plates, Tess said, "Hunter, your uncle Chip called on the house phone. He said he would really appreciate it if you would give him a call back."

Now retired, Chip and his brother Brad used to run the Bartley family house-painting business. Originally, Hunter's dad had worked with them. Esau handled random repairs while Chip and Brad did the painting.

But when Hunter was ten, his dad's brothers decided they'd finally had enough of getting Esau out of trouble and of making excuses for him when he messed up a job. They'd cut ties with their youngest brother—and by extension, with Hunter, too.

Esau had forbidden him to speak to his uncles, but Hunter hadn't needed to be told. He was loyal to his dad. He'd resented his uncles for cutting his dad loose. Hunter always used to say that he wouldn't make peace with them if they begged him to.

But he didn't seem all that self-righteous now. He only asked mildly, "Did Chip leave a number?"

"He did. It's on the message tablet by the kitchen phone."

"Great. Thanks. I'll give him a call."

Jo almost choked on her biscuit when he said

that. Never had she expected Hunter Bartley to willingly return his uncle's call.

The knock came at the front door as she was about to put Paisley in her crib. Hunter hadn't said a word about dropping by, but she knew it was him.

Her silly feet hardly touched the floor as she went to answer.

She pulled open the door and found him leaning against the doorframe, looking like exactly what he was—a hunky TV handyman, dark hair mussed just so, the sleeves of his shirt rolled to the elbows, showing off those muscled, veiny forearms of his. Beyond the porch, the shadows were growing longer. It was a mild night. The air smelled sweet, of fresh-cut alfalfa.

"You gotta help me," he said.

"Did you call your uncle Chip?"

He nodded. "That's why I need your help."

Paisley lifted her head from Jo's shoulder and blinked sleepily at the man on the front step.

He met the baby's eyes. "Hi, Paisley."

"Ack." She twisted in Jo's arms and offered him the drooled-on rattle in her hand.

He played along and took it. "Uh. Thanks."

"Ga." With a heavy sigh, she plunked her head on Jo's shoulder again.

"Come in." Jo ushered him forward. His steps

were silent behind her as she led him along the entry hall that opened into the main room. "Give me a minute. I'll just put her to bed…"

Paisley didn't make a peep when Jobeth tucked her in. Baby monitor in hand, Jo tiptoed from the room. When she turned from shutting the baby's door, Hunter was standing between the kitchen area and the living room.

She set the monitor on a side table. "You want something?" He smirked at her and gave her a once-over, those dark eyes scanning from the top of her head to the toes of her house moccasins. "Very funny," she said, deadpan. "I meant like a beer."

"No, thanks. I just wanted to talk." He stuck his hands in his pockets again and hunched his shoulders a little, a pose that said, *Nothing to worry about here. I'm totally harmless.*

Yeah, right. "Okay. Let's talk." She sat on the sectional and gestured at the chair across the coffee table.

He marched right to her and plunked down beside her. "Hope you don't mind. I have to be close to you. Really close."

"Ah. And why is that?"

"I'm feeling needy."

She tried not to laugh, but an absurd little snort did escape. "Does that work in Hollywood?"

"What?"

"Claiming neediness?"

"No idea. This is the first time I've tried it." He leaned even closer. She didn't back away. "You tell me." When his lips brushed hers, she just might have sighed. "Well?"

She let him put his arm around her, even laid her head on that broad, warm shoulder. "Hmm."

He pressed a kiss into her hair. "*Hmm* what?"

"It's like this. When you kiss me, I don't really care what you say."

"Ah." He tipped up her chin with the pad of his finger. She didn't resist. Not even a little.

Their lips met again. Her sigh was longer and deeper than before. His tongue touched hers, sweet and lazy and slow. He tasted like everything she'd learned to do without when it came to the guys she'd known—tenderness and caring. Understanding. Laughing at the same things. Trust.

The best sex ever.

Was that sad? That she'd had the best sex of her life when she was still in high school? That no one since Hunter had even come close?

Not that there had been all that many. Just Nick and a guy named Jack she'd met in college.

Easing a hand up between them, she pressed her palm to his chest.

He pulled back enough to look in her eyes. "Too much?"

"No, Hunter. Not too much. Kissing you is the best thing ever."

"But you want me to stop now?"

She nodded. "You said you needed my help with your uncle…"

"And I do." He sagged back against the sofa cushions. "He wants me to come to dinner."

"Wow. Are you going to go?"

"Yes." He reached for her.

She snuggled in close. "I have to tell you, I am impressed. I really believed you would never get near either of your uncles again."

"Well, they did turn their backs on my dad."

"Some would say they'd had good reason." Chip and Brad had paid for Esau to go rehab twice. They'd vouched for him when he started screwing up and then he'd just screwed up some more.

"Yeah. I can see their side of it, too, now, after all this time. I never would have admitted it back then, but I resented the hell out of my dad, too…"

"And yet you were always loyal to him."

"He was all I had…until you."

It occurred to her right then that if only Esau Bartley hadn't gone fishing that spring day, Hunter would never have left Medicine Creek. He would have stayed to look after his father. She wouldn't have lost him.

She used to cry at night, angry and hurt, bitterness welling within her, just thinking about how it might have been. And at the same time she'd been acutely aware of the irony that he would have stayed for the man who'd made his life so difficult, but not for the girl he loved. For a while, she'd hated him for that alone.

Now, though? She knew that life didn't adapt to the will of human beings. It was the other way around. Humans made frustrating choices and a lot of mistakes, but in the end, they adapted. If they didn't, they perished.

"Okay," she said. "So you called your uncle and…"

"He invited me to dinner. Saturday night. I said I'd be there."

"Great. Your uncle's a good guy. You'll be glad you said yes."

"It'll just be me, Chip, Aunt Latilda, Brad and Aunt Kay."

"What about the cousins and their wives and kids?"

"Just the uncles and my aunts. We'll see how that goes."

"It's going to be fine."

He winced. "I hope so."

She pulled out of his embrace and met his eyes. "Hunter, he wouldn't have called you if he didn't want to work things out with you. He's hoping to make peace, hoping that you guys can get past what happened all those years ago."

"You don't know that for sure."

"Yeah, I pretty much do. There's just no other reason for him to reach out."

"So then, will you come with me?"

"Of course, I will."

"Yeah?" He looked at her so hopefully.

"Yeah."

"That's what I needed to hear." He hauled her close again and kissed her—slow and deep this time. The taste of him excited her and the feel of his arms around her was so exactly right.

How did he do that? Be everything she wanted, and do it so effortlessly?

She ached to jump up, grab his hand and drag him to her bedroom.

But then he pulled away. "You're still waffling, overthinking this."

She relaxed and stared up at him. "I said I would go with you."

"You know exactly what I'm talking about and it's not dinner with my uncles."

"Yes, I do know." She was still measuring the pleasure he would give her against the pain she would suffer when he was gone. So far, it was a draw. Neither the promise of bliss nor the threat of her heart breaking all over again had won out.

"Sometimes it's just better not to rush in. To take my time, make sure I know what I'm doing."

"You didn't used to be so cautious."

"People change. They have to, in order to survive."

"Aw, Jo." When he reached for her again, she didn't push him away. He wrapped her in his arms.

She pressed her face into his shirt, breathed in the scent of laundry detergent and man...and thought how her idea of heaven would be if he never let go.

But he did let go.

And he always would. She reminded herself to remember that as, once again, she walked him to the door.

Chip and Latilda Bartley owned five acres a few miles north of town. They lived in a rambling white farmhouse with a wraparound front porch.

The moment Hunter stopped his pickup in the driveway, his uncles came out the front door and down the steps. They were big, husky men, both in their sixties now. Both had wide, welcoming smiles—slightly forced smiles, it seemed to Hunter.

"Why am I doing this?" he asked Jo out of the side of his mouth.

"You're making peace, putting the past behind you, letting go of pointless bitterness."

He wanted to grab her and kiss her—but then, he wanted to do that no matter what scary stuff came out of her mouth. "I'm sorry I asked." She chuckled and at least some of the tension that knotted his gut evaporated. "Stay right where you are," he commanded.

Jo had never waited around for a guy to open doors for her. Still, he loved that she humored him right now, sitting tight as he jumped out, ran around the front of the truck and pulled her door wide.

She climbed down from the seat. He barely got the door shut before his uncles converged on them.

Suddenly, the two big men looked really nervous, even shy. "Hunter," said Chip stiffly, sticking out a beefy hand. "Real glad to see you."

Hunter shook Chip's hand and then Brad's.

Brad said, "Pleased you could make it." He aimed a smile at Jo. "Jobeth, always a pleasure..."

Jo gave him a hug and then Chip, too.

"Please," said Chip at last. "Come on in."

Inside, Aunt Latilda and Aunt Kay greeted them with nervous smiles. They all sat in the front room for a bit, nibbling from a cheese platter and drinking weak vodka tonics. There was excruciating chitchat about the weather (mild), how glad Chip and Brad were to get this chance to visit with him (very) and how excited everyone in town was about his show—so, so excited.

By the time they moved into the dining room and took their seats at the long table, Hunter longed for a stiffer drink. Chip said a brief grace and Latilda served a juicy rib roast.

They were halfway through the meal when, with no warning, Chip set down his knife and fork. "Okay. I'm just going to say this…"

Hunter opened his mouth to ask him not to, whatever it was.

But then, under the table, Jo put her hand on his leg and gently squeezed. When he slid her a glance, she gave him the tiniest shake of her head.

He got the message. *Let the man speak.* He took her hand and held it.

Both of his uncles looked anxious now. His aunts had gone scarily silent.

Hunter tried to come up with the right words to reassure them that he wasn't ten anymore, that now he really could see their side. That in the past couple of years, he'd finally started to admit to himself that they must have felt as powerless as he did back then. His dad had been set on the road to self-destruction and completely unwilling to veer from that course.

Right then, Brad blurted, "We are so sorry, Hunter."

"We should have done better by you." Chip was nodding.

"And by Esau, too," said Brad. "We just didn't know what to do about him."

"And we were so mad at him." Chip raked his graying hair back with a swipe of his hand. "We let our tempers get the best of us. We took the easy way. We told him we wouldn't work with him anymore, that we wouldn't recommended him ever again—not until he sobered up and could be counted on not to chase off our customers."

"We just got fed up," added Brad. "He had problems and we knew it and we should've handled the whole thing differently."

Chip said, "He was down and we kicked him. We both thought he would be around, you know. And, at the time, Mom was there for you." He meant Grandma Daisy. "Anyway, a few weeks after the big blowup, we talked, me and Brad—we agreed we would do what we could for him when he came around again, when he asked us for help."

"But he never asked," Brad said flatly.

Hunter spoke up then. "He did have an enormous amount of pride." They all nodded at that.

Brad hung his head. "We never reached out to him."

"Well, he never did get sober," said Hunter. "Except for a little while after Grandma Daisy died. Didn't last, though."

"We felt bad for him." Brad drank from his water glass. "And we worried about you."

"But still," added Chip. "We did nothing. We didn't help him and we never found the way to protect you. It was just…"

"We gave up," Brad said, finishing for him.

Chip nodded. "Yeah, that is exactly what we did."

Hunter reminded them, "I was dead set against you. Believe me, no matter what you did, you couldn't have helped me. I wouldn't have let you."

Brad gave a sad snort of laughter. "Look at you. Defending us."

The brothers shared a glance and Chip said, "You're a better man than I am, Hunter."

"Not really. And please don't kid yourself. I did hate you both for a lot of years."

"Not surprised," Brad muttered.

"But I do remember the times you tried to reach out, to talk to me, to help me. That first year, when Grandma Daisy was still alive, you both came to see me at her house."

"Yeah." Brad scoffed. "That visit went down the crapper fast."

Hunter nodded, recalling how he'd yelled at them to leave him and his dad alone—yelled at them and then stormed out the door. By the time he finally came back several hours later, his grandmother was worried sick. "And then, after Grandma Daisy died, you both tried again. I remember you came to the cabin together..." He squeezed Jo's hand a little tighter, grateful to have her at his side right now. "As I recall, my dad accused you of turning Social Services loose on him and then ordered you off the property."

"We didn't contact Social Services," said Chip.

"But we talked about it," Brad confessed, "about trying to take you away from him, about getting custody."

"See, that you even considered such a thing would have only made me more furious with you then. But I'm a grown man now. Looking back from where I stand now, I get that my dad was a mess and in no condition to be responsible for a kid. You only wanted to help."

Brad picked up his fork as if to take a bite, but then set it back down again. "You recommended Bartley Brothers for your show. The boys were thrilled to get that job." Brad meant his son, Brad, Jr., and Chip's son, Lowell, who owned and ran Bartley Brothers now.

"Thank you," Chip said. "It's five separate jobs and it's also great for PR. The boys will be putting up pictures all over the dang internet, bragging about it on their fancy website, too."

"You didn't have to do that, Hunter," Brad said solemnly.

Aunt Latilda agreed. "And yet you did and that was so good of you."

Aunt Kay's lip was quivering. "After all you went through from the day your mom died, after the way we never worked it out with your poor dad or helped you get along in a tough situation…"

"You must have felt completely abandoned." Aunt Latilda sniffled and swiped at her wet eyes.

Jo leaned sideways, shifting toward him in her chair. Her shoulder brushed his arm. He felt a little better, just from that contact. Same as back in high school, she always knew when he needed her close.

Brad said, "Again. Thank you, for recommending the boys on your show—and even more than that, for being here tonight."

"Hey. Bartley Brothers is the best. And as for tonight, I'm very glad you invited me."

"We're just so happy and relieved that you came," said Aunt Kay.

He squeezed Jo's hand tighter, holding on for dear life. "I need to ask you something…"

"Ask," said Chip. "Anything."

"Would you have called me if I hadn't recommended Bartley Brothers for the show?"

His uncles shared a glance. And Chip said, "Yeah. But it would have taken us longer to work up the nerve."

Everybody laughed at that, including Hunter's aunts, and then he confessed, "The truth is, I was working up the nerve to call you, too. And I was pretty relieved when you beat me to it—but a nervous wreck, too, not knowing for sure what would happen when I got here."

"Oh, Hunter..." Aunt Latilda jumped up, ran around the table and hugged him where he sat. His uncles looked about as choked up as he felt.

And somehow, from then on, the tone of the evening shifted.

They left the past behind. His aunts and uncles wanted to know all about his life down in Los Angeles and they got busy filling him in on who had married whom and how many beautiful grandbabies they had now.

Before he and Jo got up to leave, they traded numbers. Hunter promised to attend a big family barbecue at Uncle Brad and Aunt Kay's a week from tomorrow.

As they went out the door, Aunt Kay said, "Jobeth, you come to the barbecue, too. I'll call your mom and personally invite her and the rest of your family."

Jobeth hesitated. "Kay, really, you don't have to—"

"Just say you'll come."

Jo sent him a look that seemed to ask *What should I do?*

He had the answer ready. "Say yes."

"Well, alright then." She smiled at Aunt Kay. "Thank you. I would love to come."

"And Paisley, too," Aunt Latilda reminded her.

"Of course."

His uncles and their wives lingered on the porch to see them off.

Hunter opened Jo's door for her. This close, he could smell her perfume—lavender and something tart. She climbed up into the pickup and he ran around and jumped in behind the wheel. They waved out their side windows as they drove away.

"Well," she said when the big white farmhouse could no longer be seen in the side-view mirror. "Peace with your uncles. That's huge."

"Yeah. I wasn't sure what to expect, but I think it went really well." He sent her a quick glance and got hung up loving how great she looked in her sky-blue dress and a denim jacket with rhinestones scattered across the shoulders.

Best of all, the dress's ruffled hem had gotten caught up beneath her thighs, giving him a nice view of her shapely knees and the sexy muscles in her calves. Her skin had that golden glow to it. He wanted to skate his fingers over her knee and down her shin to the top of her tooled dress boot… and then track it back upward on the inside, over her silky thigh.

"Eyes on the road, mister." She was hiding a grin. He could see it pulling at the corner of her mouth.

"Absolutely." He kept a straight face as he focused his gaze out the windshield again.

Jo stared out the windshield, too. But her mind was firmly focused on the man behind the wheel.

He was driving her a little bit out of her mind with those smoldering glances and that killer grin that somehow had her imagining his fingers sliding up and down her leg. She hadn't felt this revved up in years—about sixteen years, to be specific.

Her resistance to the inevitable was seriously flagging.

She glanced his way at the exact moment he slid a look at her. Prickles of awareness zipped down her spine and lifted the fine hairs along her arms.

Maybe tonight...

She really wanted to.

And she needed to get real here. No way could she hold out against him much longer. The show was scheduled to shoot well into August. That meant there were two and a half months to go before he returned to his life in LA. She would never be able to resist him for that long.

And who did she think she was kidding? At this point, she didn't even want to resist him.

Better to just get busy with it, right? Take shameless sexual advantage of him. Savor every second until he left her again. Reconcile herself to paying the price when the time for paying came.

She looked at him again—yep. He was looking right back. "Stop that."

A low, delicious chuckle rolled out of him. "You're doing it, too."

She straightened her skirt. "Well. At least I'm not driving…and wait a minute. Is this a different truck?"

Now he out-and-out laughed. "You only noticed just now?"

"Don't mock me. Answer the question."

He faked a straight face. "Yes, Jobeth. Your sister almost had a baby in the other one, so I traded it in."

She remembered then. "Oh, I get it. That's why you had that blanket on the seat when we left the hospital Tuesday night."

"Right. How's Starr doing, anyway?"

"Going stir-crazy staying at home. I don't think she can stand to take it easy much longer. She'll pack up the baby and head for her office at the *Clarion*, where she'll get right back to work. Don't be shocked if she shows up when you're taping the show, baby on one arm, laptop tucked under the other."

"I won't be the least surprised." He sent her another quick, hot glance. "Starr only has one speed and that is full speed ahead."

Tonight. She wanted it to be tonight—wanted *him.* She couldn't stop thinking about how much.

But then again, she had to pick up Paisley at the main house. How would that work? Would he come in with her and then follow her right back out again? Or just wait in the truck as she went and got the baby from her mom and then headed for her place with Hunter rolling along behind her?

No. Uh-uh. It was all too awkward and weird.

Yes, she'd admitted to herself that she would end up in bed with him.

Just maybe not tonight.

When he pulled to a stop at the base of her mom's front walk, she said, "Good night, Hunter."

He gave her one of those long, burning looks. "Where are you going?"

Had he forgotten she had a baby? "It's not even fully dark yet. I'll just run in, get my little girl and walk to my house, no problem. You can go ahead and park your truck."

"No way. Get Paisley. I'll take you to your house."

"Don't be silly." She pointed at her place. "It's right there. A two-minute walk, tops."

"Okay, Jo." He said it softly, tenderly. With a

huff of breath, she met his eyes…and melted a little inside. "Thanks for going with me." His slow, warm smile made her long to reach for him, yank him close, kiss him endlessly. "It turned out great, but I really was afraid it wouldn't. It meant a lot to have you there just in case things went sideways somehow."

"I was glad to do it." She hooked her little purse securely on her shoulder and grabbed the door handle. "You are not to get out just to open my door."

He gave her a smirk. "Have it your way."

"Good night, then…"

He gave her a nod as she jumped down.

Her mom was waiting just inside the front door. "Kay Bartley called me twenty minutes ago. Big family barbecue at her place a week from Sunday. We're all invited—your dad, Edna, Brody, Ethan John—and so I am assuming that the evening went well."

Jo grinned. "Yes, Mom. Things went well. Very well. Hunter reconciled with the uncles and we're going to party hearty at Kay's house."

"I'm so glad."

"Me, too." Jo asked, "How was Paisley…?"

"An angel."

"But with attitude."

They grinned at each other and Tess said, "Yep.

That's our girl. I put her down at seven. Not a peep since then."

They went upstairs together to the room Tess had fixed up just for Paisley. The baby didn't wake when Jo gathered her close.

Back downstairs, she kissed her mom's cheek. "Thanks, Mom. You're the best."

"You know I love to have her. No need for thanks."

Outside, the shadows had deepened. There was no sign of Hunter or his truck. He might have driven around to the garage, or maybe he'd just gone back into town to have a drink with some of the TV people.

Paisley sighed softly and nuzzled her sleepy head against Jo's neck. Jo cuddled her closer as she headed along the driveway.

In the empty house, she carried Paisley to her room. The baby hardly stirred as Jo tucked her in.

When she emerged into the main room, she couldn't decide what to do next. By turns, the evening had been tense and tender, happy and so very sad. She felt at a loss now. Wandering into her bedroom, she sat on the edge of the bed to take off her boots and socks.

DC came out from under the bedside chair.

"Come on." She clicked her tongue at him. "Give me the sugar." He meowed in his cranky way as she scooped him up and cuddled him. For a moment, he allowed her attention and even granted her an almost inaudible purr. But then he was squirming, ready to get down.

"Fine, then. Be that way." She let him jump to the rug. He stretched, yawned and headed off toward the short hall that led to the main room.

Once he'd disappeared, she just sat there, staring through the open door of her bathroom. She wished that she'd been a little braver with Hunter tonight—bold enough to go for a kiss. Honest enough to simply say *Come on over to my house. Stay...*

Instead, here she sat, shoulders slumped, staring into the walk-in shower at the far end of her bathroom as she idly fiddled with the hem of her dress.

It was still early. She should get comfy in her sleep pants and her favorite floppy sleep shirt, climb into bed and watch a movie or read until she fell asleep.

Ugh.

Boring. She could be kissing Hunter right now. But instead, she sat on the edge of her bed trying to decide what to do with herself for the rest of the night. She needed to...

What was that?

Something had struck the window behind her—bits of dirt, maybe. Or pebbles.

Startled, she shot a glance over her shoulder.

Hunter stared at her from the far side of the glass. Grinning, he lifted his hand and tossed another fistful of pebbles at her window.

Chapter Eight

Hunter couldn't wait to take her in his arms. He crooked a finger.

She mouthed, *Seriously*?

At his shameless nod, she rose, rounded the end of the bed, marched to the window and slid it open. Now only the screen kept him from climbing over the sill to get to her.

"Take off the screen." When she scowled at him, he added wistfully, "For old time's sake?"

"You could end up badly injured if my dad or one of the hands happened to see you peering in my window and took a shot at you."

"They never caught me before. Take off the screen. Come on. It's romantic."

She made a show of folding her arms under her breasts and looking at him sideways. "You know, it's just not the same if you don't have to climb that hackberry tree like you used to." Back then, her room had been upstairs in the main house. He used to climb that damn tree a few times a week, at least.

He flattened his nose against the screen. "Jo-beth, I have to work with what I'm given. Let me in. Please."

She heaved a big, fake sigh before relenting and removing the screen.

"Thank you." He swung a leg over the sill and boosted himself inside. "Allow me." He held out his hand and she gave him the screen, which he slotted back into the window frame. After sliding the window shut, he pulled the curtains closed. "Now," he said, turning to her, making a show of brushing imaginary dust off his hands. "That wasn't so tough, was it?"

"Oh, Hunter…" All of a sudden, her eyes looked enormous…and wet with tears.

Not the reaction he was going for. "Wait. What'd I do? Are you crying?"

"Shut up." She threw her arms around him.

Okay now, this was more like it. Her soft breasts pressed into his chest and her slim waist felt made to fit his hands. Wrapping her close, he lowered his mouth to hers.

They kissed for the longest time. He savored the taste of her as they stood there by the window, holding on to each other like they would never, ever have to let go. It was perfect, his arms full of her, his mouth on hers, his head reeling with her clean, fresh scent.

The kiss went on, unbreakable, as he walked her backward to the bed. He pushed that glittery jean jacket off her shoulders, then slid his hands down over the perfect curves of her hips to get hold of the frilly hem of that blue dress. He started to gather it up in his fists.

But then she jerked her mouth away and pressed her palms flat against his chest. "Wait."

He growled low in his throat. "You know you're killing me here."

She met his eyes. "I don't have condoms. I mean, I'm on the pill, but still I think we need to…"

He stopped her with a finger to her soft lips. "No problem. I've been carrying two in my wallet for weeks now." Because damned if lack of protection was going to be the reason she said no when they were finally getting somewhere.

She laughed at that. "You sound so determined."

"You have no idea." He pulled out his wallet, took both foil pouches, set them on the nightstand and put his wallet away. "Fair enough?"

With a naughty smile, she took the hem of her dress in both hands.

"Hold on."

"Hmm?"

"Do me a favor. Take that off nice and slow."

Her smile promised him everything. "Like this?" She lifted that little dress inch by sweet inch.

He felt kind of dizzy in the best possible way. "Exactly like that."

She got it. She remembered how much he liked it when she took it slow. And so she did just that. She made it last, revealing those sleek thighs first and then the curves of her hips. She wore little white bikini panties, nice and snug.

Upward that little dress went, the hem fluttering, over the delicate shape of her ribs and those breasts, two pretty teardrops, covered in white satin. Too soon, the dress hid her flushed face as she pulled it up the length of her arms.

The blue fabric fluttered over her head, pulling her hair with it for a moment before the gleaming strands spilled to her shoulders again. She drew a slow, shaky breath as she dropped her arms to her sides and the dress drifted to the floor.

"Hey," he said.

"Hey." They shared a smile.

He *had* to touch her. One step and he was where he needed to be. He lifted his hand, rested it carefully on her silky shoulder and then let his palm drift down the outside of her arm. "It's been way too long…"

Her breathing had changed, become careful, measured. She licked her lips.

He took her in his arms again.

They kissed some more, long, searching kisses, as their hands roamed freely. It felt so good, so right, to be learning the smooth, strong shape of her all over again.

He wanted more. He wanted all of her.

Maybe that would never happen.

But for tonight, everything felt possible. Right now, she was his and he belonged to her and whatever happened later, she was every promise fulfilled and all of his dreams made real.

No matter what tomorrow might bring, tonight they were bonded, their connection solid. True.

"Too many clothes," he muttered.

"Suddenly, you're impatient," she taunted with a bad-girl smile.

"You bet I am."

"Hey." Stepping out of the circle of his arms, she shook a finger at him. "I just want to point out that you're the one still wearing all your clothes. I, on the other hand…" Grinning, she reached behind her and fiddled with the hooks back there. Then she eased the straps off her shoulders one-by-one, pressing her free palm to her chest to hold the bit of satin in place. When she spread her arms wide, the bra dangled from one hand. She let it go.

He tried to reach for her, to pull her close again.

"No, you don't." She took another step back... and then she shimmied out of those little white panties.

"Jo..." It came out as a croak.

She braced her hands on her bare hips and clucked her tongue at him. "How is it that you're still fully dressed?" He started to reach for her again. She slapped his hand lightly and then moved close once more. "No touching," she warned. "Not yet. Keep your hands to yourself and let me help you out of your shirt."

"You're just trying to drive me out of mind."

"Oh, yes I am." She went to work undoing the buttons down the front of his shirt. He'd rolled the sleeves to his elbows, so she only had to ease the shirt from his shoulders and it fell away. "Hunter..." Her voice was sweet and low and sort of wistful as her hands drifted out over his shoulders, down his chest, along his belly to the buttons of his fly, where he was aching to be set free.

Longing flooded through him. It made his eyes burn, his throat hurt and his stomach clench. All these years, and for most of them, he'd never dared to dream he might end up in a bedroom with this woman again. All these years, and somehow, here they were.

Whatever happened later, at least he would have the memory of this night. He held his breath and fisted his hands at his sides to keep from grabbing her.

She lowered her gaze and chided, "You still have your boots on." He stifled a groan as she took him by the shoulders and pushed him down to sit on the bed.

Swooping to a crouch, she pulled off one boot and then the other. She was the most tempting thing he'd ever seen, naked on her knees before him, struggling to get him out of his boots.

When she fell back on her ass, laughing, cradling his second boot, he refused to wait another second. "Stand up."

She set down the boot and eyed him warily.

But then he coaxed softly, "Please."

She bit her plump lower lip, studying him. And then, finally, she rose. He stared at her face as he tore off his socks, jumped to his feet, whipped off his belt and shoved down his pants and boxer briefs.

They gazed at each other.

She looked as amazed as he felt. In a dazed whisper, she asked, "Is this really happening?"

"Yeah. Finally." He grabbed for her.

She grabbed right back, shoving her mouth up to his, moaning a little as he speared his tongue beyond her lips. With one leap, she was on him, wrapping her arms and legs around him, kissing him like she would never let go.

The bed was right there. He turned and laid her down on it. Stretching out on top of her, he took care to put most of his weight on his arms.

As for Jo, she was all over him. Holding on tight, arms and legs twined around him, her mouth plastered to his, she refused to break their long, sweet kiss, though he ached to crawl down her body. He needed to explore every inch of her, every sweet, secret curve.

Groaning out a rough laugh, he reached back and got hold of both her wrists. She kept on kissing him at the same time as she tried to shake off his grip.

Not happening. They were both laughing as they struggled—laughing between sighs and hungry moans.

When he finally pressed her wrists to either side of her head, she glared up at him. "Not fair!"

He kissed the tip of her nose. "You're so beautiful, Jo."

"Sweet words will get you nowhere." She wrapped her legs tighter around him. His aching erection pressed way too close to where he longed to be…soon.

But not yet.

She was strong, but he was determined. He took her mouth again and she sighed, softening beneath him.

When he moved downward, she didn't fight him—not too hard, anyway. She let him kiss his way over the sweet terrain of her body, taking his time, making love to every inch of her. He lingered at her breasts, drawing her rosy nipples into his mouth, swiping his tongue around them as he sucked them.

By then, her teasing resistance had melted to tender cries and soft sighs. He licked his way down the center of her, dipping his tongue in her navel, pausing to nip at her hip bones just to hear her gasp.

And then she pleaded, "Please, Hunter. Anything… Yes, that. Do that. Oh, please…"

Words seemed to desert her when he settled between her thighs. She made soft, eager sounds as he kissed her, stroking her with his fingers, nipping with his teeth, latching on and then softening the pressure, giving her the flat of his tongue.

When she came, she reached down and speared her fingers in his hair, pressing him closer, holding him right where she wanted him. He wondered for a second or two if he might suffocate—wondered and then laughed deep in his throat because…hey. What a way to go.

For a while, they didn't move. He rested his cheek on her belly. Idly, she combed her fingers through his hair.

And then she reached out a ha..d for the nightstand. He lifted his head and saw her grab one of the condoms.

"Here." He tried to take it from her.

But she held it out of reach. "Let me."

He flopped to his back. She got up on her knees and straddled him. He groaned at the sight of her above him, hair every which way, cheeks and throat flushed red, breasts swaying as she bent close to roll the condom down over him.

So. Many. Years.

Everything was different—and yet, in this, between him and Jo, it felt the same. Urgent and beautiful. Painful and sweet and dirty. Open.

True.

She rose up to her knees, her hand down between them, holding him where she wanted him.

And when she eased him inside her, she held his gaze.

Until he filled her all the way, deep and hot and so, so good. He groaned and let his eyes drift shut. Taken by her, cradled in her body's soft heat, he drowned in pure pleasure.

"Look at me, Hunter. Give me your eyes."

With effort, he did as she commanded. They stared at each other.

Slowly, he smiled. Her mouth bloomed wide in answer.

And then she started to move.

The world flew away. He reached up, wrapped his arms around her and hauled her down tight against his body, rolling them, topping her.

"Oh, yeah…" She breathed the words into his kiss. "Just like that…"

And they were moving together, waves in their own private ocean, lost to everything but each other. The years fell away and it was only the two of them, as they had always been, Hunter and Jobeth, together, bound.

Heart to heart.

"I went to your cabin more than once after you left," she said softly. "I used to sit on the front step and cry. That was in the first year you were gone. It was boarded up. I wondered what would happen to it, with you so far away."

It was after eleven. They sat up against the pillows. He had his arm wrapped around her and she rested her head on his shoulder as she tried not to wish that he would never leave, that it could always be this way for them.

"It's still there, still mine," he said. The cabin was up in the mountains, west of town. "I paid the property taxes, which weren't a whole lot but put a strain on my limited funds the first few years. Then, after I started on my first show, I contacted a property manager in Buffalo to look after it."

"Have you been up there since you came back to town?"

"Not yet. But I'll get around to it."

She wanted to ask if he would let her go with him. But right now, they had other things they needed to talk about. She felt his lips in her hair, his warm breath flowing over her skin.

Tears blurred her vision and tightened her throat, same as they had the times she stood alone outside the empty cabin after he'd left her. She swallowed them back, though she yearned to give in to them.

But she wouldn't cry. She would love every minute with him for as long as it lasted, and when he had to go, she would not try to hold him.

As though he'd read her thoughts, he said, "I came back here wanting to see you again, to make it right with you, somehow. I wanted to work things out with my uncles, too."

She couldn't resist reminding him of that other reason. "And rub a bunch of noses in your success."

"That, too—and as I've already admitted, I was wrong about that."

"Because you were always a hero in Medicine Creek."

"Maybe the word *hero* is a bit over-the-top."

"Not the way I see it."

He slanted her a wry look. "I do have a point I really need to make…"

She wrinkled her nose at him. "Well, alright, then. Go on."

"I, uh…"

She leaned her head on his shoulder. "It's okay. Just say it. Just put it out there."

He touched her chin. She looked up into his eyes. "Jo, LA is my home now. I have a life there, and work I love. I'm going back as planned. I can't see myself changing my mind about that."

Her throat got tight from all the emotions tangled up inside her. She drew a slow, careful breath and said, "I know. And I will stay here. This ranch is *my* home."

"I never expected otherwise."

"My dad said you would be here until sometime in August."

"That's right. Maybe as late as September, depending on what disasters crop up. They always do, no matter how hard we work to anticipate all the crap that can go wrong."

"Three months or so, then."

"Yeah."

It wasn't near enough. But a lifetime wouldn't

be enough, so she would take what she could get. "Okay."

He was quiet. Finally, he asked, "Okay? Just like that?"

"Yeah. Move your stuff over here from the main house. Stay with me for as long as you're in town."

His hard arm tightened around her. "You're sure about this?"

She laughed. It felt good. They would need to laugh together a lot and to make the most of every moment they had. "Don't get too excited. Remember, I have a ten-month-old. She requires a lot of attention and sometimes she still wakes up in the middle of the night and won't go back to sleep."

"I think I can handle living in the same house as Paisley." He kissed her, lightly. With something like reverence. And then he said, "It's more than I ever dared to hope for, to be here like this with you when for so long I believed I would never see your face again…" She wished he would leave it at that. "But Jo, I—"

"Stop."

"What?"

"When you're done working here, you're going back to LA. I get it and I can live with it."

"What about your folks?"

"What about them? My mom and dad know how to mind their business. Don't worry. They'll be fine."

"I don't want to cause trouble."

She snort-laughed at that one. "Yeah, the horse has left the barn on that one. You're nothing but trouble—the best kind. Because you're worth it."

"Jo…" He tipped up her face with a finger and kissed her again. "I do want to be with you. If you'll have me."

"Yes. I will have you—fair warning, though. Most days, I'm up at four thirty."

"I keep early hours, too. We can have breakfast together."

She leaned closer and whispered in his ear. "As long as you're cookin'."

"You're going to love my western omelet."

"Can't wait. And speaking of morning…"

"I know." He pressed his lips to her cheek and then gently scraped his teeth against her skin, sending prickles of sweet sensation shivering all through her. "We should get some sleep."

They plumped their pillows and she switched off the light.

Turning on her side to face the window, she had a feeling she would never drift off. Her body seemed to hum with the echo of so much pleasure. And her mind wouldn't settle down. She wanted this time with him and she would have it. She knew she would suffer when it was over.

But then he snaked an arm around her and tugged her in against him, spoon-fashion.

She smiled into the darkness. Because it felt good, to be here with him. It felt exactly right. Some things were too good to say no to.

And this, now, with this man?

It was one of those things.

Chapter Nine

"He's good with her." Tess sipped from her tall glass of iced tea.

Across Kay and Brad Bartley's big, unfenced backyard, Hunter stood at the grill next to Brad, Jr. He had Paisley in his arms. She was waving her hands and babbling away—giving him orders, no doubt.

In the week that he'd been staying at Jo's house, Paisley had talked to Hunter a lot. Most of what she said made no sense, but Hunter always played along. She would point at things and he would hand them to her.

Sometimes she would crawl right up to him, drag herself to her feet by grabbing two fistfuls of his pants leg and then bounce up and down as she grunted, "Uh! Uh! Uh!" until he scooped her into his arms.

"They do get along," Jo said to her mother. "I was kind of surprised. That I know of, Hunter's never been around kids all that much. But he's patient and sweet. He treats her like a little princess."

"She *is* a little princess," her doting grandma replied. And then she frowned—a tiny frown, but Jo saw it.

After all, she'd had her entire life to learn how to read the expressions that flitted across her mom's face. "What, Mom?"

Ice cubes rattled as Tess took another sip. "Don't look at me like that. I'm your mother and I'm just... checking in."

"At the Bartley family barbecue?"

Tess winced. "You're right. We should talk later, in private."

"Mom. You're freaking me out here."

Her mom looked really sheepish. "Sorry?"

"Too late to back down now. Just say it. Please." *Put me out of my misery.*

"I just want reassurance..."

"Okay..."

"That you know what you're doing, I guess."

Jo thought of her dad, then. He'd seemed fine with Hunter moving to her house. Had she read him all wrong? It hurt to think that her dad might disapprove of her actions. Since she first came to know him when she was seven years old, she'd wanted only to please Zach Bravo, to be like him— steady and true, someone to look up to and count on no matter what. Careful to keep her voice down, she demanded, "Does Dad need reassurance, too?"

With a bewildered little shrug, Tess shook her head. "Strangely, no. He's happy to see you with someone you care about, however it works out in the end. He warned me to keep my nose out of it."

She hadn't realized she was holding her breath until relief had her letting it out in a rush. "You should have listened to him."

Her mom stood taller. "I did listen to him." She spoke softly—just between the two of them—but firmly, too. "And now I'm doing what *I* think is best. Honey, what if Hunter refuses to move back home? Are you going to move down there to Hollywood to be with him?"

"He's not moving back home, Mom."

"Ah," said Tess. Probably because she had no idea what else to say.

"He's not moving home and I'm not moving to LA. We're spending some time together. That's what this is."

Her mom's eyes got huge. "But…" She seemed unable to find the right words.

"Just say what you're thinking, Mom. It's okay."

Tess eased an arm around her and pulled her close. "I'm on his side," Tess whispered. "I'm on *your* side. But it all seems a lot more real since he moved into your house."

"It *is* real, Mom."

"I'm just afraid this is going to break your heart all over again."

She leaned her head on her mom's slender shoulder. "This time with him? It's what I want." Hunter glanced her way then. She gave him a warm smile. He grinned right back at her as Paisley tried to chew on his ear.

"He's looking at us," her mom said.

"No kidding. Smile back."

"I am." Tess fell silent. For a moment, Jo dared to hope that the conversation was over. But it wasn't. "I just want you to be happy."

"And I *am* happy. Right here. Right now."

"What about Paisley? She's already growing attached to him."

Jo had thought that over. Yes, Paisley might miss him for a while when he left. But she was very young and he wouldn't be with them for that long. Her memory of him would quickly fade. "Mom."

"Yes?"

"I've thought it through. All of it. Being with Hunter right now is a choice I've made and I'm happy with that choice. I'm not changing my mind."

"You're stubborn. Always have been."

"I love you and this time with Hunter is what I want. I can deal with the consequences, I promise you."

"I just needed to be sure. And, honey, I love you, too. More than words can ever say."

"That was…" Hunter brushed at Jo's tangled hair with his fingers, smoothing it off her forehead, thinking how right it felt to be here, naked, with her. "Words fail me…" They were both breathing hard.

"The best," she agreed with a husky chuckle.

Panting in unison, they fell back to their separate pillows. He stared up at her bedroom ceiling, thinking that he hadn't been this happy in a long time—not in sixteen years.

Strange, really. Growing up, he'd hated his life…except for when he was with Jobeth, just the two of them. Talking. Making love. Sitting on a blanket out by Crystal Creek under the stars. His moments with this woman were the best of his life.

Going up on an elbow to bend over her, he dropped a quick kiss on her soft lips. "Be right back."

"Promises, promises."

A few moments later, he rejoined her in the bed.

She rolled toward him and he kissed her again—a light kiss, but a long one. When the kiss ended, they stayed close, face-to-face, their noses inches apart. He fiddled with her hair as they stared at each other, grinning.

"It was a good day," he said. "Everyone seemed to enjoy it."

"They did," she agreed. "I had a great time."

"I'm meeting my cousins at Arlington's for happy hour on Wednesday."

"I approve."

He hesitated, wanting to strike the right tone.

She groaned. "Whatever it is, just say it."

So he did. "Everything okay with your mom?"

She rolled onto her back again. "Why?"

Now he knew for sure that they'd been talking about him. "You two seemed to be having an intense conversation…before dinner? While Paisley and I were hanging out at the grill with Brad, Jr.?"

"We were just touching base."

"About?"

She shook her head at the ceiling. "Why do I get the feeling you already have a pretty good idea of what we talked about?"

"It was about me, right? About how I'll go and you'll stay and that will be hard on you."

She braced up on her elbow and propped her head on her hand. "Yeah. So what?"

"What did you tell her?"

"That I want this time with you and you want time with me and we'll deal with the future when it gets here."

"And she's against that, right? What about your dad? Is he against us being together, too?"

"Whoa. Slow down."

"Just answer me."

"She's my mother. She doesn't want to see me get hurt."

He got that, he really did. He dialed back the defensiveness. "Sorry. Your mom's been good to me. I feel like I messed her over, somehow. Like I came here under false pretenses... I don't know."

"Hunter, she knows how we were, you and me, when we were together all those years ago. She knows that what we had was strong. She was here when you left. She saw how much I missed you. Both she and my dad knew that you and I might connect again if you came back to town, especially if you stayed right here at the ranch. But they invited you to stay here, anyway. They are not judging you, I promise you. My mom was just checking in with me, making sure I'm being honest with myself."

He reached for her. She went into his arms, turning, snuggling back against him. Breathing in the clean scent of her shampoo, soothed just to hold her close, he whispered, *"Are* you being honest with yourself?"

She laughed then, the sound low and so sweet. "Where is this conversation going? Because I believe we've already covered this ground—and thoroughly, too."

"Yep. But just a yes or a no would be really great right now."

She squirmed around to face him. "Yes. I *am* being honest with myself. And what I would love more than anything is if I don't have to start missing you when you aren't even gone yet."

"Jo…" *I love you. I will always love you.* But it felt wrong to say that. A man had no right to declare undying love when he knew that in a few months he would be walking away.

She dipped close and kissed him. "Let it go, Hunter. Be with me now. That's what I want most of all."

Hunter took Jo's request to heart.

He spent every free moment with her and Paisley. Some nights, they had dinner at the main house. Zach and Tess treated him with fondness and respect. If sometimes he saw a shadow of worry for her daughter in Tess Bravo's dark eyes, he did what Jo had asked of him. He let it go.

They had fun together, him and Jo, including a Saturday picnic under the trees at their favorite spot along Crystal Creek. Twice, he took her out to dinner, once to a really good Italian place in Sheridan and once to Arlington's.

The night they went to Arlington's, they ran into Mel. Hunter introduced them. Mel was charming and friendly and left them alone after a few minutes of chitchat. He couldn't help hoping that the producer had finally seen the light and would stop badgering him to put his private business on *Rebuilt by Bartley.*

But then Monday, she was on him the minute he showed up for taping at the library. "So…you and Jobeth Bravo, hmm?"

"Mel. Don't go there. I mean it."

"An old flame rekindled. I love it."

"Did you hear what I just said?"

"We only want a little interview with her. Brief, I promise you. A bit of background on what it was like growing up with you here in Medicine Creek."

"No."

"But—"

"No interviews with Jobeth. Not happening."

"Well, you are certainly protective of her. It's sweet, really."

"How many ways can I say this, Mel? Forget it. You got my cousins on tape. That's enough." Brad, Jr. and Lowell had been only too happy to be interviewed for the show. And when Mel prodded them for personal information about Hunter's life growing up, they stuck with the facts—that his mom had died when he was small and he'd been raised by his dad. They'd said that his dad was also a handyman and Lowell had joked, "So now you know. Hunter comes by his skills honestly."

Mel had also talked Zach, Carmen Amestoy and Mrs. Copely into a series of Q and A's. He'd seen those interviews. Jo's dad, the gift-store owner and the librarian had kept their answers simple, positive and brief. Mel and David had plenty of material to put his growing-up years in context. They didn't need more.

But Mel thought they did. The woman was nothing if not relentless. "Hunter, that you're spending time with a local girl is terrific—and that you were a couple years ago? Our audience will love that."

"Mel, listen carefully. Not everything I do is about pleasing our audience. Some things are private, pure and simple."

Luckily for him, Starr strolled in right then with her baby hooked to the front of her in one of those baby wraps and her trusty laptop under her arm. Mel rushed over to greet her and Hunter made his escape.

He watched the producer fawning over Jo's sister and thought how the days were flying by much too fast. All of a sudden, it was the middle of June. He'd been living with Jo at her house for almost a month. Time. He wished he could lasso it and wrestle it to the ground.

He really did need to go take a look at the cabin. He would probably sell it and the five acres it stood on, or so he'd been telling himself for sixteen years now. Maybe if he walked through it one more time, he could finally let it go.

Really, there was no rush. He had 'til the end of August or even September to drive up there and… what? Say goodbye? To a pile of logs and a bleak childhood? Hadn't he left all that behind long ago?

Friday night, while Jo put Paisley to bed, he sat out on her front porch watching the shadows creep over the crests of the mountains off to the west, beyond the main house. The door opened behind him. Jo came out and settled on the step beside him.

"I need to go up to the cabin," he said, eyes on the gray mountains. "I keep putting it off."

"How about tomorrow? You, me and Paisley?" He reached out a hand. She put hers in it. "We'll make a day of it," she said. "Weather's supposed to be warm and sunny. We can go swimming after…"

"Come here." He tugged on her hand.

With a soft laugh, she slid even closer. Neither of them said a word after that. They watched the sky turn orange along the crests of the mountains as sunset came on.

In the morning, he and Jo put on swimsuits

under their clothes. They packed up Paisley and her baby gear and headed for the cabin. It wasn't a long drive, but to Hunter, it sure felt like it.

In the back seat, Paisley babbled and crowed for the first fifteen minutes and then suddenly went silent.

Jo glanced over the seat. "Out like a light."

They shared a smile.

Not much later, he took the turn onto the narrow dirt driveway that led into the trees. When he rolled to a stop in a small clearing, the single-story log cabin waited straight ahead.

"It looks good," Jo said.

He nodded. The roof was intact, the windows to either side of the door unbroken, the yard and the porch free of debris.

In the back seat, Paisley woke with a cry. "Maw-maw!"

Jo got out, took her from the car seat and rubbed her back until she settled and rested her dark head on Jo's shoulder. By then, he was standing beside them.

Paisley lifted her head and babbled out a flood of almost-words as she reached out her chubby arms for him.

He handed Jo the key to the cabin and took the baby. Paisley was small and soft and solid. Holding her in his arms reminded him that he was the grown-up now. Years had gone by. The boy who'd once lived here was no more.

"Lead the way," he said.

Paisley pulled on his ear and tried to grab his nose and talked nonstop as he mounted the steps to the front door. Holding her close helped—her chatter kept him grounded as a grown man, dependent on no one but himself.

Jo unlocked the door and pushed it open onto a shadowed main room with a kitchen sink and a bit of counter under the window on the side wall. On the opposite wall, a narrow hallway led into darkness, but he knew what was back there—a tiny bathroom straight ahead and two small bedrooms to either side.

"No furniture," Jo observed.

"I had the property manager get rid of it." Too many memories—not to mention an open invitation to rodents and other pests.

Paisley made a soft, contented sound. She'd rested her head on his shoulder again. He put his hand on her warm little back and reminded himself that he didn't live here anymore.

Jo flicked the light switch. "No lights."

"I had the utilities turned off before I left for California," he said, thinking that really, there'd never been anything in this cabin to hurt him, not in a physical sense. Nothing except loneliness and the constant fear that his silent, unhappy father who fell into a drunken stupor every night and often in the daytime, too, would disappear on him someday, leaving him with nothing and no one to hang on to. "There should be a couple of battery-powered lanterns in that cabinet to the left of the sink."

Jo got one of the lanterns. She turned it on and a warm glow filled the dim room.

Paisley lifted her head and pointed at the light, letting out a flood of happy babble, after which she put her head back down on his shoulder with a big sigh, as though keeping things upbeat right now took a whole lot of effort. He nuzzled her cheek and she cooed at him, a comforting sound.

"Well?" Jo gave him a bright smile. "Let's check out the other rooms."

At his nod, she led the way through the door to the hallway, where they entered one empty bedroom and then the other. They peered into the tiny closets and then gave the bathroom a look. The whole tour took three minutes, tops.

When they emerged into the main room again, Jo asked, "What now?"

It all felt so completely anticlimactic. "I don't know..."

She turned off the lamp and stuck it back in the cupboard. They went out the door and Jo locked it up again, dodged around him and sat on the edge of the porch.

Paisley lifted her head and gave him a puzzled look as he sat beside Jo. "Ah-dee-baw?" the baby asked.

"Just having a little sit-down," he explained. He turned her around and set her on his lap.

Jo took a rattle from her back pocket and shook it. Laughing in delight, Paisley grabbed for it. "It's all yours, sweetie pie." Jo handed it over and Paisley set to work chewing on it.

He leaned toward Jo. "Well?"

"It's pretty much what I expected."

"Small, dark and empty, you mean?"

She leaned her head on his shoulder. "It's a log cabin in the woods. You did have furniture back then, right?"

"We did."

"And the lights would have been on. It's not all that awful."

He shrugged. "It was dark, even with the power on." He kissed her, quick and hard. "Thanks for coming here with me."

Paisley reached for Jo. Hunter passed her over to sit on Jo's lap. She made a low, crooning sound and tapped her rattle on her own leg.

Jo asked, "So will you sell it?"

"Can't say. I don't want to be here, but for some reason, I can't give it up."

She met his eyes. "And there's no reason you have to until you're damn good and ready."

"I may never be ready."

"And that's just fine, too."

He knew exactly what she was thinking. Despite how tough his childhood had been, he remembered his dad with love and hesitated to let go of his only connection to the man. "Don't psychoanalyze me."

"Wouldn't dream of it."

He stood. "Come on. Let's go swimming."

She lifted Paisley to her shoulder and followed him to the truck.

They returned to the Rising Sun and their favorite swimming hole on Crystal Creek. She'd brought Paisley's travel play yard. They set it up under a cottonwood tree not far from the creek bank and Paisley played with her toys while they swam. When she got fussy, Jo gave her a bottle. She lasted another hour before she started fussing again. They packed up the truck and headed for the house, where Jo put her to bed.

Out on the back deck, they grilled steaks and shared a nice bottle of wine. Later, Jo led him to her room.

It was so good with her, natural. Right. As each day passed, he had more and more trouble imagining himself leaving her when the show wrapped.

He'd started indulging himself in unrealistic ideas—that he somehow might convince her to move to LA. She could keep horses in California.

He had the money now to buy her a place in the country—a nice piece of property in Hidden Valley or maybe Somis. They would build a house and stables. She could ride every day. Paisley would grow up with all the advantages—the best schools *and* a rural lifestyle, too. Plus, he could teach them both to surf.

They could make a good life.

Except that she would be a thousand miles from home and from the family she loved so much, from her life on the Rising Sun.

Monday, *Rebuilt by Bartley* was filming right there at the ranch. When Jobeth finished her morning chores, she peeked in at the bunkhouse just to see what was going on.

Melanie Huvey, the producer, spotted her before Hunter did. The woman hustled right over to say hi. Actually, Jo kind of liked Mel, as she insisted Jo call her. Mel was pushy and single-minded, yeah.

But she looked you in the eye when she started pushing. With Mel, the agenda was right out there in the open. "Okay, so Hunter says no way, but I'm still wondering if you might be willing to do a short interview for the show, to talk to us a little about how you met Hunter and what he was like back when you were growing up."

Before Jo could answer, Hunter came striding toward them looking superhot in his snug

T-shirt, jeans and tool belt with a scowl on his face. "What's going on?"

Jo couldn't help but laugh. "You look like the top of your head is about to pop off. Settle down."

He turned to Mel. "We discussed this."

Mel stood right up to him. "I realize that. But it never hurts to ask."

"You did ask. I said no."

"Hello?" Jo waved her hand in front of his face. "This might actually be *my* decision, don't you think?"

"Jo, I'm just trying to protect your privacy."

She smiled at Mel. "Could you give us a minute?"

"Absolutely." With a big grin and a firm nod of her head, Mel Huvey left them alone.

Jo turned to Hunter. "I know you're working. Sorry to barge in."

He braced his hands on his hips and shot a hard look at Mel, who'd stopped across the gutted main room and started whispering intensely with a tired-looking white-haired guy in horn-rimmed glasses. "You're welcome to stop by and see me anytime," Hunter said. "And I'm sorry about Mel. Sometimes she just won't take no for an answer."

"I'm guessing that's kind of her job."

He seemed to relax a little. "She doesn't freak you out?"

"No." Jo put her hand on his arm and leaned

close. "How about this? Put her off for now. We'll talk about it tonight."

He was scowling again. "It's a bad idea."

"Hunter."

"What?"

"We'll discuss it. Tonight."

"I can't believe you're even considering it."

Was she? At this point, who knew? But she didn't want him getting some idea he needed to protect her from the people he worked with. She could stand up for herself just fine. "Tonight." She planted a kiss on his scruffy cheek and left before he could say anything more.

That evening, he got back to the house at a little after six. They had a beer. She'd had stew simmering in the slow cooker all day. They ate and hung out with Paisley and DC for a while and then Jo put the baby to bed.

When she emerged into the main room, he was waiting for her, DC sprawled on the sofa next to him. The cat jumped down and headed for the kitchen area and Hunter patted the space the cat had vacated.

"You are looking way too serious," she teased, hoping to lighten the mood a bit.

He took her hand and laced his finger with hers. "I guess I am. I don't want anything messing up our time together. Mel getting a hold of you for the show could go off the rails in so many ways."

"I don't get it. You said they can't put anything in the show about your private life that you don't want to share."

"That's right."

"Well then, if I say things you don't like or that bother you somehow, you can make sure they get cut."

"It's not really that simple. True, you're going to get a bunch of softball questions. *Rebuilt by Bartley* is not *Dateline*. But you never know what they'll ask until they ask it. What if they ask you questions that upset you? What if you give the interview and then change your mind about it? There are so many ways it could turn out to be a bad experience for you. Our time together is too damn short. I am not saying yes to anything that might get between you and me."

She didn't like that he was trying to make her decision for her. But she did see his point. "You really don't want me to do it, do you?"

"No, I don't. They know we're seeing each other and they're loving the romance angle. They're going to ask you how we met. What went on between us back in high school? How we broke up? They'll want to know if it's serious now and will you be moving to LA with me? Jo, you need to ask yourself, do you want all that on TV?"

Did she? "I don't know."

He huffed out a breath. "How can you not know something like that?"

"It's just not a big secret, you and me. Everyone in town knows that we were in love and you left and I didn't go with you. It's not a new story. It's two kids in love wanting different things from life. They go their separate ways. It's sweet and it's sad and I was really broken up about it for a long time."

He cleared his throat. "Me, too." The words came out rough and low.

She rested her head on his shoulder. "But the years went by and we both survived and nowadays I focus on how good it was between us, how happy we were together."

"And you and me and how happy we were, that's nobody's business."

She wanted to grab him and hug him and… soothe him somehow. But first, they needed to get down to the real issue here. "So the truth is, *you* don't want them to interview me."

"Haven't I made that completely clear?"

"Just confirming—you've got issues behind putting me on TV to talk about us. To me, well, the more I think it over, the more I see that it's no big deal. I would be…local color. And that's fine with me. It's good for your show and it's good for Medicine Creek. We're becoming something of a tourist destination, you know. A little PR never hurts."

He narrowed his eyes and peered at her suspiciously. "You're just so relaxed about this all of a sudden. Are you sure you're the same girl who wouldn't get near me for the first three weeks I was in town?"

"I'll have you know it was two weeks. And that I got over it." She slanted him a sideways glance. "I'm guessing they're going to be interviewing my dad and Starr."

"And several others, too."

"You don't seem worried about *them* holding their own."

He raked back his hair. "They're not you. I said it before. There's a chance it could go sideways and that would get between you and me. And I don't want anything getting between you and me."

"Hunter."

"I hate it when you say my name all patiently like that."

She pressed their joined hands against her chest. "Look at me—come on."

With clear reluctance, he met her eyes. "What?"

"How long until the millions of people who love your show will even see this interview I would do…if I do it?"

"Jo…"

"How long?"

"Several months, at least."

"Hunter, you won't even be in town by then.

There is no way my consenting to be interviewed on your show is going to come between you and me because by then, there will be no you and me."

He flinched as though she'd slapped him. And then, yanking his hand from hers, he jumped to his feet and headed for the door.

"Hunter, wait a minute!"

He kept walking. A moment later, he was out the door, pausing only to shut it behind him.

Chapter Ten

Jobeth grabbed the baby monitor and followed.

But when she got outside, he was nowhere in sight. She stood on the porch and debated her next move.

She didn't want to go searching for him. Partly because she didn't want to get out of range of the baby monitor...and partly because whatever was chapping his butt, he wouldn't have run off if he didn't want to get away from her right now.

So alright, then. He needed alone time? He could have it.

Because she'd learned a few things about relationships during her disastrous marriage to Nick. One of them was that running after a guy and demanding that he communicate with her rarely went well.

Back in the house, she went to her room. In her bathroom, she filled the jetted tub with water, tossed in a bubble bar and took off her clothes. After anchoring her hair up in a messy bun, she climbed in for a long, soothing soak in a giant froth of bubbles. The water was hot. Leaning back, she closed her eyes and tried to think relaxing thoughts.

She must have dozed off.

When she opened her eyes, Hunter was sitting on the edge of the tub. She gasped in surprise at the sight of him. Water and bubbles sloshed on his jeans and overflowed to the floor as she sat up. "Hunter! What the...?"

"Sorry." Those dark eyes of his were tender now. "Sorry that I took off like that, and that I scared you just now. I know we agreed that it would be over with us when I leave town. I know I'm acting like a jerk. But it hit me hard, what you said—that by the time the show airs, there'll be no us."

She reached for him. He didn't duck away, so she laid her wet hand against his cheek. The bubbles got caught in his neatly trimmed beard. "I'm sorry, too. It was mean, the way I said it."

"But it's the truth." He turned and pressed a kiss into her palm. "And I don't want to think about it."

"Me, neither." She brushed the bubbles from the side of his face. "So let's not think about the end. Let's focus on right now, on the time we have together."

"It's a deal." He studied her face for a long, quiet moment and then asked, "Do you still want to do that interview?"

"Yeah. I think it's good sometimes, to do stuff I'm not completely comfortable with. And don't worry. I promise to say only wonderful things about you."

He chuckled. "Okay, then. I'll tell Mel it's a go and give her your number."

"Great."

"And I've been thinking…"

She leaned up. He met her halfway for a slow, sweet kiss. "Thinking what?" she asked against his parted lips.

"The second week of July, I need to fly to LA for six days. I have some meetings I can't put off. Also, the executive producer of my show is throwing a party at his house in the Hollywood Hills. I promised I would make an appearance."

She felt forlorn at the thought—but it was only six days, she reminded herself. He would be back in no time. "I'll miss you."

"Well, that's the thing. I don't *want* to miss you, not even for six days." He gave her his best smile, the crooked one that always made her feel a little swoony. "I'll be missing you enough when I leave town for good."

She scooped up a handful of bubbles and blew them at him. "No more sad talk. I can't take it."

"My point is, please come with me."

"To Los Angeles?"

"Yes, to Los Angeles. It's just six days. It's only a few meetings I need to deal with and then that party. The rest of the time, it will be you, me and Paisley staying at my condo in Malibu. We can hang out on the beach right there, go to Disneyland, whatever you want to do. You might want to try surfing. It's five miles along the Pacific Coast Highway from my place to Zuma Beach."

"And that means what?"

"There's good surfing at Zuma Beach."

"I don't know. Paisley is getting to that age where you can't just stick a bottle in her mouth when she gets cranky. She's got a mind of her own and yet she still has to have a regular schedule. I think it will be a few years before she's ready to appreciate a trip to Disneyland."

"Then maybe she could stay with your mom while we're gone?"

Paisley would definitely be fine with her mom. But the trip itself seemed…dangerous, somehow. To enter his everyday world, to stay at his place with him. Like they were testing the waters for a longer commitment or something.

And they weren't.

They knew where they stood and that wasn't going to change. No way would she be moving to Malibu.

He didn't look happy. "You don't want to come with me."

Objectively, it seemed wrong to go, somehow. Like she would be crossing some invisible line. But then again, he was here, in her world. Why shouldn't she spend a few days with him in his? "Let me think it over."

His expression relaxed. "Can't ask for more… and you're getting goose bumps."

She laughed and rubbed her arms. The water had definitely cooled. "I'm starting to feel prune-y, too— can you hand me that towel?"

He got up, took a fluffy bath towel from the rack and held it up for her. She stood, shivering a little now. Stepping out of the tub, she turned so that he could wrap the towel around her. His lips brushed the curve of her neck. "Damn, you look fine in nothing but bubbles."

"Play your cards right, mister. You just might get lucky tonight." She rested her head back on his shoulder and tipped up her mouth. He took it.

The kiss went on for a while. It felt so good, his warm arms around her, his lips playing on hers.

"Let's get you dried off." He took his time about it, rubbing the nubby towel down her arms, along her sides, over her hips and between her thighs.

By the time most of her was dry, she was moaning.

"Let's go to bed," he whispered as he scooped her high against his chest. She wrapped her arms around his neck and kissed him as he carried her to the other room.

"I knew it," Mel gloated when Hunter gave her Jo's phone number. "This is great. I'll give her a call and we'll try to do the interview this week."

"I bet you will. Give me the paperwork. I'll run it by my agent."

"Hunter, we're hardly going to ask her to sign her life away. It's a boilerplate, one page long."

He nodded. "So do you want the interview or not?"

"Fine. I'll email it to you today. You're so protective of this woman," she groused. "It's cute, but annoying."

"Thanks, Mel."

She sent him the short contract an hour later. He forwarded it to his agent, Estelle Smart, who did him a favor by looking it over and getting right back to him.

After reminding him that she was only giving her personal opinion and not legal advice, Estelle said, "It's simple and direct. Nothing to worry about. Unless she was hoping to get paid, which she won't."

"She's not expecting money."

"Well, then, what else is there to say, except see you next month?"

He thanked her and they hung up.

Friday, they taped Jo's interview out by the horse barn in front of a picturesque wooden fence. A couple of handsome horses grazed in the background. It was sunny, with a slight breeze that teased at Jo's hair, worn loose on her shoulders for the occasion.

Elinor, of hair and makeup, had spent twenty minutes fiddling with Jo's makeup and primping her hair. Hunter thought she looked great in jeans, dress boots, a green silk shirt and a locket on a gold chain that her dad had given her.

She did fine when the cameras rolled, too— didn't even seem nervous as she chatted about her life on the Rising Sun. She spoke easily of their relationship in high school and then said how happy she was to get to spend time with him while he was in town for the show.

That evening, Tess took charge of Paisley. Hunter and Jo went out for dinner at the Stagecoach Grill.

"See?" Jo teased him as they ate barbecued chicken and steak fries. "The interview went great."

"No second thoughts?"

"Nope. I think it was fine."

He was nodding. "You're a natural."

She raised her glass of white wine to him. "Oh, yes I am. Plus, I really like this green shirt. I'm proud to show it off on TV."

He teased, "You'll have your own show before you know it."

"I don't know. I'm pretty busy. I really don't have time for stardom."

"It could happen. Be prepared."

They laughed together at that.

He waited until later, back at her place, to bring up the trip to LA.

They were in the bedroom. She'd just taken off her pretty green shirt.

He went ahead and asked again, "So will you come with me to LA next month?"

She stood there holding her shirt, looking way too uncomfortable. "I do appreciate your inviting me, Hunter. But I have work I need to do here and I just can't—"

"Yeah, you can."

"No, I really don't think so."

"Six days, Jo. Come on. We only have so much time together and I don't want to waste a day of it."

She pressed the shirt to her chest. "Hunter, I just don't think—"

"It's six days. Say yes." Did he sound desperate? He felt that way. "Come with me."

"No, really. I can't."

"You *won't*." He knew he sounded like some sulky little boy—so what? He wanted her with him, damn it. "We both know you can get away. If you want to."

"It's just better for me not to. It really is."

"Why better? That makes no sense."

"I really don't want to give any signals that I might be willing to move to California."

"For God's sake, I know that."

"I don't want to give *myself* signals that somehow we will make it work, together, for real. For a lifetime. Think about it. We need to keep things in perspective. It's not a bad idea to have a few days apart, you know?"

Yes, it was a bad idea. A completely crappy idea.

Fury flared inside him. He almost headed for the door, same as he'd done Monday night.

But what good would that do...except to put distance between them? He didn't want distance. He wanted her closer. Storming out would get him the opposite of that.

He dropped to the edge of the bed.

It took her several seconds, but she came to

him. Carefully, still carrying the green shirt, she sat down beside him.

"Sorry," he said.

She leaned her head on his shoulder with a sweet little sigh as he thought how six days seemed like a lifetime, every moment of which he would miss her and hate being apart from her. If that was "perspective," he would eat his own tool belt.

Still, he didn't want to fight. And he wouldn't waste another minute of their time together trying to get her to do something she just didn't want to do. "Alright." He schooled his voice to mildness. "You're not coming with me. I get it, I understand."

"Thank you. For letting it go." She tipped up her chin. He looked in those ocean-blue eyes of hers. She gave him a trembly little smile.

It was all the invitation he needed. He took the green shirt from her, tossed it to the bedside chair and wrapped her up in his hungry arms.

Monday afternoon, Jo dropped in on Starr at the *Clarion*.

Her sister was sitting at her desk, writing an article about water conservation with one hand while holding a nursing baby Cara on her other arm. She'd come back to work a week before. Jerry Espinoza was still helping out, but Starr was right where she wanted to be again—running the show.

"I keep thinking I should slow things down with Hunter," Jo said.

"Slow things down?" Starr shot her a dismissive look.

"What is that look you're giving me?"

"Don't get snippy, little sister."

"Me? Starr, you're the one getting snippy."

"Well, I mean, why would you slow things down? You and Hunter are having a fling, right?"

"It's not a fling," Jo argued. "It's, um…"

Starr made a big deal of tapping her foot. "Waiting…"

"It's way too intense to be called something as casual as a fling."

Starr typed out a flurry of words one-handed and then replied, "Flings by nature are often intense. Also, it's *like* a fling in that it's not meant to last. When he goes back to his life in Los Angeles, you're done."

"Maw-maw-maw!" Paisley was standing on her own chubby feet over by a bookcase on the inner wall. "Maw-maw-maw!" She called out for Jo as she bounced up and down, two plump fists held high.

Jo laughed. "We'll, aren't you the bouncy one—and standing all on your own, too."

"Dah!" Paisley managed two steps before plunking to her butt.

Jo applauded. "Good job!" She turned to her sister. "Did you see that?"

Starr beamed. "First steps?" At Jo's proud nod, she added, "And I was here for them."

Jo went to Paisley, scooped her up and kissed her. "Good job, honey. Good girl!"

Paisley babbled out something incomprehensible and then demanded, "Dow!"

Jo put her down. Paisley dropped to her butt and grabbed for the plush elephant Starr had given her right after Cara was born. Flopping onto her back, she set to work chewing on the poor thing's mangled trunk.

Jo stared at her, amazed at how fast she was growing. She couldn't wait to tell Hunter that her baby had taken her first steps that very day.

Hunter. She sighed. "I think I'm in love with him." She hadn't really meant to say that out loud.

"Duh," Starr replied.

Jo whirled on her sister. "You did not just *duh* me."

"Yeah, I pretty much did. Want to talk about it?"

Jo pressed her lips together. "Not really…"

"I'm here," her sister said. Starr's voice was gentle now. "I'm ready to listen."

"I know. And I'm grateful that you are. But admitting I'm in love with him out loud? That's enough for right now."

They left it at that as, on the floor, Paisley dropped her stuffie, got to her hands and knees and crawled over to Starr's desk. She pulled herself upright and then cooed out a few almost-words.

Starr bent over her nursing daughter to give her niece a quick kiss on the tip of her nose. "This is your cousin. Her name is Cara." Paisley watched Starr's mouth move with great interest. Starr said, "Ca-rah. Ca-rah."

"Ca-ca-ca," Paisley replied. "Wa-wa!"

"You are getting there, my darling. Good job." She glanced Jo's way again. "I can't believe she'll be a year old next week."

"I know." Paisley's birthday was the Fourth of July. They would celebrate at the Bravo family's Independence Day barbecue. "It feels like yesterday that I got to hold her for the first time and now a whole year has flown by."

"Time tends to do that," Starr replied softly. "And listen…"

"Hmm?"

"Don't throw away the time you do have with Hunter. Just don't do that, Jo. Give yourself up to it. Drink it down like fine wine. Nothing's forever. Make some beautiful memories to keep you smiling as the years go by."

Later, as Jobeth drove her pickup home to the

ranch with her little girl snoozing in the back seat, she thought about her sister's advice.

When exactly it had happened, she couldn't say for sure, but over the past two months, she and Hunter had become a real couple again.

Just because it would end in August or September didn't make what they had together any less real. She admired him so much. She wanted him. She trusted him. She loved the way he was with Paisley—tender and attentive, encouraging and fun.

She loved sharing breakfast with him early in the morning and then knowing that he would try to get home in time for dinner at night.

She loved just being with him.

She loved *him*. Loved him a bone-deep way, a way she couldn't imagine ever loving anyone else.

And if they didn't have a lifetime, well, Starr had made a good point. Jo needed to love him full-speed-ahead for every day she had with him.

No. She wouldn't tell him, wouldn't say she loved him. That would just feel like putting pressure on him to stay…or on herself to go with him when he left for good.

She wouldn't say the words. But she would hold them in her heart.

She would live them, day by day, for as long as she had him at her side.

* * *

The time, Hunter decided, was flying by much too fast.

All of a sudden, it was the Fourth of July…and Paisley's first birthday.

The day dawned humid and overcast. But by noon, the big bowl of the sky was a gorgeous, cloud-free blue.

Zach and Tess hosted the Bravo family barbecue in the yard at the Rising Sun. All the Bravos showed up, including Zach's cousin Nate and his wife, Meggie, who owned a nearby ranch, the Double-K. Nate and Meggie arrived with their grown kids Jason, Sarah and Joseph.

Cash and Abby came in from town with their kids *and* their grandkids. Starr and Beau brought the whole family, too—Lizzie, who was home from college for the summer, and Sawyer and Cara. And dear old Daniel Hart.

Just about everyone arrived with a gift for the birthday girl. At two in the afternoon, Tess brought out the birthday cake. Paisley, enthroned in her high chair, which Jo had set outside for the occasion, managed to blow out her single candle… with a little help from her grandfather. She ate her cake with her bare hands and a lot of enthusiasm.

Hunter had a great time catching up with everyone. Around four, Tess took charge of Paisley.

Jo and Hunter headed for the Bartley family get-together at Uncle Chip's place. They hung around at Chip's until dark and then drove into town to Patriot Park, where the chamber of commerce had hired a band and erected a portable dance floor.

Hunter took Jo in his arms and they danced beneath twinkle lights strung from tree to tree. By then, he'd accepted the fact that she wouldn't go with him to LA the following week. He was focusing on loving every minute he did have with her.

Reluctantly, he let her out of his arms for the fast numbers, but pulled her close again whenever the music slowed. Around midnight, the band struck up a cover of Alan Jackson's "Remember When."

It was a perfect moment—him and Jo, holding on to each other, swaying to a song about love and forever and time standing still. He found himself thinking that this, right now, was happiness.

And then it got even better.

She put her soft lips close to his ear and said, "Hunter, if you still want me to go to LA with you next week, yes, I would love to go."

His heart stopped…and then started racing. "Jo. You sure?"

"Yes."

"Hot damn!" He kissed her then. He couldn't stop himself. She kissed him back, long and sweet and deep. Right then, it seemed to him that time really did stand still. The dancers swaying around them, the band, the other folks enjoying the warm evening at the picnic tables nearby—they didn't even exist.

There was only him and Jo, wrapped in each other's arms, swaying to a country song under a sky full of stars.

Chapter Eleven

"This is over-the-top, it really is." Feeling giddy and excited at the prospect of the six days to come, Jo raised the glass of champagne the flight attendant had just served her.

"But nice." Hunter touched his glass to hers. "And so comfortable." He sat back in the plush seat.

The company that produced Hunter's show had provided a private jet for the trip to and from Los Angeles. The interior of the jet resembled nothing so much as a space-age living room—a living room occupied by not only Hunter and Jobeth, but also Melanie Huvey, David Reid and the smiling flight attendant.

"It *is* nice," she agreed and had another sip

of bubbly goodness. "But I feel a little bit guilty drinking champagne at five thirty in the morning."

"Guilt is not allowed. Not today. That's a hard-and-fast rule."

"Says who?"

"Me. And I ought to know. I just made it up."

She laughed and drank more champagne. Out the window, the sun was coming up on the horizon, light chasing off the shadows.

"Hey."

"Hmm?"

"I'm really glad you came, Jo."

They shared a smile and she replied, "Me, too."

A few minutes later, the flight attendant served them all coffee and eggs Benedict.

At Santa Monica Airport, two cars were waiting. Mel and David shared one. The other car whisked Jo and Hunter off to Hunter's two-bedroom condo on the Pacific Coast Highway overlooking Escondido Beach.

His place literally took her breath away. It wasn't large, about sixteen hundred square feet in total, but it was gorgeous. Perched on palm-covered bluffs above the beach, the lower floor had an open plan facing a long deck overlooking the jewel-blue Pacific. The kitchen had a blue granite island and charming old-fashioned tile on the other counters. The appliances were state-of-the-art.

She opened the fridge. "Fully stocked. And everything is spotless…"

"That's Yalena's doing. She's an all-around miracle worker. She shops for me, cooks several meals a week for me and keeps everything clean." He grinned at her. "Life is good, you know?"

"I can see that."

"It's a long way from my first LA apartment," he said as they leaned on the waist-high wall that embraced the deck. Down the hill, past the tumble of vivid dark pink bougainvillea, the ocean glittered in the sun.

She leaned his way. "Tell me about that first apartment."

"It was a studio in the Valley. One room with a hot plate and a sofa bed—and a bathroom I could barely turn around in. Not that I cared. I was on a big adventure. The only problem I had then was the constant ache of missing you."

She met his eyes. "I missed you, too. So much." *And too soon, I'll be missing you again*, she thought but somehow managed not to say. A change of subject was in order. "Speaking of bathrooms, I love the old tile in this place. Like from some perfectly restored bungalow—those big, square tiles and the borders of flowers and waves and seashells."

He nodded. "I like it, too. When I first saw the listing online, I marveled that none of the previous owners had chosen to get rid of the original tile. Gotta respect that."

And there was more to love about Hunter's condo. You could walk out the back gate and take four stone steps down to the pool. From the pool level, another stone stairway wound through lush foliage to the private beach below.

That day and that evening, they didn't go anywhere. They hung out by the pool and down on the beach. They shared dinner on the patio at the restaurant next door and made love in his big bed for hours.

She woke up the next morning feeling oddly disoriented—so far from home in this beautiful subtropical paradise by the ocean.

"I miss my baby," she said as he cooked her breakfast in sweats that hung low on his hips, showing off all those fine handyman muscles of his. Really, he reminded her of some impossibly perfect male model on Instagram. Even his dark, thick hair was spiked just right on top. She didn't care much for beards as a rule, but he kept his short and neatly trimmed. Lately beards looked a lot better to her than they used to.

He plated a western omelet and set it in front of her. "Eat and then call your mom."

"I'm going to need a long FaceTime session with Paisley."

"Sounds like a plan."

As it turned out, the video chat with Paisley lasted five minutes. Paisley bounced around shouting "Maw-maw-maw!" and trying to lick the screen of her grandma's old iPad. After about three minutes of that, she only wanted to crawl down off the sofa and find something more interesting to do.

Tess laughed. "She's a busy girl."

"I miss her." Jobeth couldn't help sounding a little bit sulky. "I'll call tomorrow. And Mom, don't hesitate to reach out if there's anything I can—"

"Sweetheart. We are all fine here. You know I'll be in touch if it's the least bit necessary."

"Thank you."

"In the meantime, you guys have fun."

Hunter leaned over her shoulder. "We will. Thanks, Tess."

Her mom gave him a glowing smile and they said goodbye.

That day, while he was off at some meetings in Century City, Jobeth met Yalena, who was tall and shapely and could have been anywhere from thirty to fifty. She had a big, glowing smile and she whipped around the condo, dusting and straightening.

Before she left, she asked Jo for any special instructions—things she wanted done a certain way or any foods she might desire.

"Yalena, I've got nothing I need right now that

you haven't already provided. Just keep doing what you're doing."

"I will! But anything you want, you write it down on the pad in the kitchen, eh?"

Jo promised she would and Yalena swept out like a queen, head high, hips swaying.

Hunter wasn't due back for a couple of hours yet. He'd left her the keys to one of his cars, but she really didn't feel like braving the Los Angeles traffic.

Instead, she put on her swimsuit and went down to the beach, which was every bit as peaceful as the day before. Just a few random sun worshippers and a couple of dog walkers.

She spread a towel on the sand, slathered on sunscreen and tried to enjoy the moment. But she kept thinking of all the work she should be doing on the Rising Sun. Long, lazy days at the beach weren't really her style.

A shadow fell over her. "Why are you frowning?"

She cracked an eye open and stared up at Hunter, who was looking superhot in a pair of blue board shorts. "Just thinking how lazy I'm being. I should be working. You know, ditches to burn, horses to train, alfalfa to bail..."

"So driven. It's good I brought you to the big city, where you can relax and take it easy for a few days."

"Humph. Did you enjoy your meetings?"

"As meetings go, they were fine—too long but at least somewhat productive. And let's not talk about work."

"Fair enough."

He held down a hand. She let him pull her to her feet and they ran out into the shallows together, where they splashed each other wildly and she jumped on him and dunked him, after which he returned the favor.

The next morning they were up before dawn. Hunter presented her with a spring suit—a wet suit with short arms and short legs suitable for Malibu water temperatures in July, he explained. They headed north on PCH to Zuma Beach, where he gave her a surfing lesson and she tried to catch a wave—just a little one. She managed to get up once and then quickly wiped out. Hunter swore that was a triumph for a first-timer.

She was grinning when they got back in his Range Rover.

"You enjoyed yourself," he said about her surfing attempts. "A lot."

She asked, "Can we do it tomorrow?"

"See how you feel at four in the morning."

"It's a deal."

Like the day before, he had meetings. Jobeth did FaceTime again with her mom and her little girl. It went about the same as it had yesterday. Her daughter had minimal patience for communicating via electronic device. Paisley slapped at the iPad a time or two, kind of trying to break it open and get to her maw-maw inside.

"How's DC doing?" Jo asked before they said goodbye.

Tess grinned. "Same as always. I go over there to feed him and he takes his time coming out from under the sectional. Then he lets me pet him if I'm lucky."

"I miss him."

"I'm sure he misses you, too."

"No, you're not. And neither am I."

When Yalena breezed in, Jo was more than eager for company. She followed the housekeeper around shamelessly, asking her questions about her life in LA.

Yalena said, "I work. I go home. The next morning, I get up and work some more—and you should go shopping, I think. Buy some beautiful clothes. Keep busy, eh?"

"I hate shopping."

"Well, what do you *like* to do?"

"Hmm. I like to go out on an icy winter's night to check on the stock and see the aurora borealis painting the sky. I enjoy riding up into the mountains and camping out under the stars."

"That first thing, I can't help you with. For camping, you could maybe try Big Bear."

"It's lunchtime, Yalena. Have a glass of wine with me."

"Jobeth Bravo, you are a bad influence."

"I try."

They laughed together…and Yalena went right back to work. She was long gone when Hunter returned at five.

The next day was Saturday. Hunter had no meetings, just that fancy party of his in the evening. Jo felt great—the aches and pains from her first surfing lesson were minimal—so they got up good and early and drove to Zuma Beach. She popped up twice. That was fun.

Later, Hunter wanted to take her shopping. She tried to beg off, but he said, "Come on. I want to spoil you."

She had very little interest in being spoiled. As for the party, she already had a dress and flat sandals she'd brought from home.

But now she'd started to wonder if her simple summer dress was going to cut it. "Tell me the truth. This is some big, fancy party, right? And you're going to be wheeling and dealing, or whatever you do. I really don't see any reason why I have to go with you."

"Please go with me." He looked at her with those velvet-brown eyes full of hope and affection.

"Don't look at me like that."

"Please. I want to buy you a pretty dress and show you off."

"Oh, this is not going to go well."

They went to Beverly Hills, where he insisted on buying her a sexy blue silk dress she loved on sight. He also sprang for a gorgeous pair of fancy shoes that she hoped she wouldn't have to wear for more than a couple of hours, tops.

Back at his house, Yalena appeared—with hair products and a makeup kit the size of a suitcase.

Jo laughed. "Yalena! You do hair and makeup, too?"

"I have—how should I say it—many talents?"

And she did. Three hours later, Jo had a killer mani-pedi, hair that flowed like a waterfall to her shoulders and just enough makeup to highlight her best features.

Hunter tipped Yalena hugely and sent her on her way. Then he turned to Jo. "You look beautiful."

Jo was feeling more doubtful by the moment. "'Beware of all enterprises that require new clothes.' Didn't Thoreau say that?" They'd read *Walden* in English class junior year.

"Could be—and I mean it. I'm almost sorry I

bought you that dress. Now I just want to get it off you."

"If we stayed here, that could be arranged."

"Don't tempt me. We're going."

Hunter had two parking spaces in the basement of his building—one for his fancy SUV and one for a sleek silver-gray Porsche Carrera 911.

They took the Porsche for the hour-long ride south to Santa Monica and inland, gradually working their way up into the Hollywood Hills and to Mt. Olympus, a gated community where all the houses looked straight out of *Architectural Digest*.

Hunter's gorgeous car carried them up a curving private driveway to an ultramodern white house with giant windows that looked out over the rugged hillside and down into the smoggy city below. When he pulled to a stop, the valet was waiting. Hunter gave him the key and took Jo's hand to lead her inside, where everything was white, black or gray—there was even a white grand piano where a gorgeous brunette was playing something soft and jazzy.

The main floor opened up to expansive balconies and decks on three sides. In back, giant glass doors opened onto the pool area—and not just one pool…oh, no. There were three, each on a different level, and wide terraces with stair steps down the side of the mountain, each level furnished with plush lounges and padded, inviting chairs, bringing the outside in.

Jo grabbed a flute of bubbly wine from a passing server's tray and strolled around with Hunter, who introduced her to people whose names she promptly forgot. Hunter was so sweet, though. He talked her up in the cutest way, announcing with real admiration and pride that she was a rancher and a horse trainer, the best that there was.

The way he looked at her made her heart rate speed up. It hit her all over again, this time harder than ever before—like a punch to the center of her chest, one that stopped her racing heart midbeat.

She was completely and hopelessly in love with him. And she'd been lying to herself for weeks now, reassuring herself that she could have him for a little while and then just let him go all over again.

He introduced her to their host and the creator of his show. Terry Sloane was tall and fit with ebony skin, a broad, strong nose and the eyes of a hawk. "I've seen the tape of your interview, Jo-beth. You've got presence and a certain…inner calm, which I very much admire. I hope to see more of you."

She didn't even want to think what he meant by that, exactly. It wasn't as though she would become a regular on Hunter's show or anything. Too soon, Hunter would be leaving her for good and she really, really hated how bleak she felt every time she thought about getting through the days without him.

And what did it matter, what Terry Sloane meant, anyway? It was probably just one of those things that people said.

She smiled and thanked him and kind of wondered how she'd gotten here, hanging on to Hunter, facing how completely she'd fallen in love with him again, as sweet music flowed out from the white piano and beautiful people milled all around them.

Terry Sloane was still standing there, still regarding her with those sharp dark eyes. "Bravo is an important name in Los Angeles. Any relationship to Jonas Bravo?" Jonas Bravo was a legendary figure. Partly for his wealth and his genius in business, but also for his tragic past. When Jonas was only a boy, his father had been attacked and killed in his own home. His baby brother had been kidnapped from his crib. Jonas had walked in on the kidnapping and been seriously injured. The baby vanished, lost forever, everyone assumed… until years and years later.

"I've never met him," she said. "But Jonas Bravo and my father are third cousins. They share the same great-grandfather, John Bravo, who was the original owner of the family ranch, the Rising Sun."

The producer's eyes twinkled like black stars. "I just have to ask. I've heard that Jonas is related to Evan Bravo-Calabretti, Prince Consort of Montedoro..." Montedoro was a gorgeous principality on the Mediterranean Sea.

"Again, my father is the prince's third cousin. It's a big family, really. And no, I've never met the prince, either."

"Fascinating," said Terry Sloane.

Jo debated explaining that she was adopted and not biologically related to either of those famous Bravos, but it just felt like way more specific information than Terry Sloane could possibly want or need.

And, anyway, she was too busy having an internal emotional breakdown trying to accept the fact that Hunter was starting to seem more important to her than the life she loved on the Rising Sun.

Which was impossible. Too painful to even consider.

She would never leave her own life behind. It mattered—her roots in Wyoming. Her life on the Rising Sun, the solid ground she'd found at last after her birth father died.

And what about Paisley? How could she possibly tear her baby girl away from the grandparents she adored. Paisley needed to grow up with family all around her. Family mattered—and keeping family close gave a child security and a true sense of belonging.

Someone tapped Terry Sloane on the shoulder and those hawklike eyes turned elsewhere. Mel and David appeared. Mel was grinning from ear to ear. Turned out there was lots of buzz for *Hunter Comes Home*. Network executives had attended screenings of selected segments from the future limited series and the response had been enthusiastic across the board.

The four of them wandered out to the pool area, where a few brave souls had stripped down to skimpy swimwear and stood around sipping umbrella drinks. In one of the pools, several of the women had climbed onto the broad shoulders of some very hunky guys and started a chicken fight, resulting in a whole lot of splashing, laughing and shrieking.

Jo stepped back from the action before her dress got soaked and accepted another glass of champagne. She promised herself this would be the last one and swore on a large imaginary stack of bibles that all thoughts of being utterly, overwhelmingly, desperately in love with Hunter stopped right now.

A Hollywood party in a white mansion with gorgeous bikini-clad women chicken-fighting in the pool was challenge enough for her country-girl soul. She didn't need to make it harder by drinking too much. And she certainly had no intention of getting maudlin over whether or not she would be able to tell Hunter goodbye.

"Hunter!" A hot redhead in a floaty white dress came striding toward them. Jobeth stepped back as the woman flung herself at Hunter. "Imagine seeing you here!"

"Lauren, hi." He gave her a perfunctory hug and then let her go as Jo remembered where she'd seen the woman before—in Hunter's Instagram feed during her embarrassing stalking sessions after she'd learned he was bringing his show to Medicine Creek.

The woman kept her arms linked loosely around Hunter's neck as she beamed up at him. "Am I over-the-top?"

"A little." He reached out a hand for Jo. Numbly, she linked her fingers with his. He pulled her closer. "Jo, this is Lauren Maris."

Lauren sighed. "It's true. I'm the ex." She finally stepped back as she aimed a slow smile at Jo. "And you are Hunter's hometown girl." She really didn't sound bitchy or mean.

Still, it was hard not to hate her. Lauren Maris was sleek, sophisticated and gorgeous, a woman in her element, one who belonged in Hunter's world…and she had recognized Jo on sight.

He must have told her everything…

And why did that hurt so much? He and Lauren had been married, for heaven's sake. Of course, he would have told her all about the girl he left behind.

"Hi, Lauren. Good to meet you." Jo looked the other woman directly in the eyes and smiled.

"So. You two have reconnected, I see."

As Jo tried to decide how to reply to that, Hunter beat her to it. "Yes, we have."

Her heart kind of melted…maybe. A little. He had his arm around her now. She let him pull her closer.

"So cute," said Lauren. She might even have been sincere. Who knew? Jo reminded herself that she didn't know this woman and whatever Lauren Maris thought of her was none of her business. "Hunter, I wonder if I could steal you away just for two minutes?" Lauren turned that glittering smile on Jo. "You'll have him back before you know he's gone, I promise."

Hunter wasn't buying. He pulled Jo even closer. The warmth of his body reassured her. "It's a party, Lauren. Not now. As I said yesterday, I'll be in touch."

He would? A sick wave of jealousy swirled

through her. In touch about what? And wait… Had he spoken to this woman yesterday? Had one of his meetings been with her?

Lauren was watching her. "Just business," she said, as if in answer to all the questions swirling through Jo's head as her heart beat an aching tattoo under her ribs and her face felt as if it was on fire.

Was she flushed tomato-red?

Pride took control. She gave Hunter a gentle push. "Go ahead. I'll be right here."

He looked down at her, frowning. "Jo…"

"Go on." She raised her empty glass. "I'll get myself some more delicious champagne and enjoy the party." She tipped her head high and made a shooing gesture with her fingers.

Lauren's white teeth flashed with her smile. "Thank you, Jobeth. Two minutes. On my honor…" She took Hunter's arm.

As Jo watched them walk away, she couldn't help thinking how right they looked together, two beautiful people, at home here in a way Jo doubted she could ever be.

With no real desire for a refill, she set her empty glass on the tray of a passing server.

Hard reality was no fun at all. But she did need to face it.

She was deeply in love with Hunter all over again—and nothing had changed. It was still going nowhere with him. Somehow, she'd positioned herself right back where she'd ended up with him sixteen years ago.

His life was not her life.

And her heart? It was breaking, same as before.

"This is about Lauren, right?" Hunter demanded when they entered the condo after the silent ride home from Terry's party. He was feeling a little bit guilty. He really should have told Jo ahead of time that one of his meetings had been with his ex-wife.

But he'd been a coward, hadn't wanted to do anything that might possibly get her worrying over some imaginary lingering attachment between him and Lauren.

"Hunter, it's okay. I *liked* her. Really." Jo sounded sincere. But her eyes told another story.

He'd hurt her and now she'd shut down on him. *Way to go, fool. Now she definitely thinks you've got something going on with Lauren.*

Jo turned away from him and headed up the stairs to the bedroom level. He hesitated by the kitchen island, trying to decide how to make this right. She was out of sight before he followed.

"Come on. Wait up…"

He found her in the master suite, standing at the floor-to-ceiling windows that faced a balcony and a view of the ocean beyond.

She turned to him. "So. We might as well hash this out, huh?"

"Jo, please…"

She put up a hand and he stopped in midstep. "You had a meeting with her yesterday, I take it?"

"Yeah. She had an idea to run by me. A new show she wanted me to think about helping her develop."

In two steps, she reached the end of the bed, where she sat and took off her shoes. "And?"

"I heard her out because you never know. It might have been something I really wanted to do."

"Was it?"

"No. It's not for me. I told her so yesterday. But Lauren is nothing if not persistent. So I told her so again tonight. That's it, all that happened, I promise you."

"Hunter…"

"What?"

"Why didn't you just say you were meeting her?"

He dropped into a chair across from her. "It felt awkward, I guess. Because I used to be married to her. I didn't want you to think there was anything going on between her and me, you know?"

She smiled sadly and shook her head. "It's better to be honest right up front. It might cause some tension between us, but this, right now, knowing you met with your ex-wife for any reason and hid that from me… Well, I'm kind of disappointed I have to explain why that would bother me."

He felt like a dick—probably because he'd behaved like one. "Yeah. I can see that. I tried to make things…easier."

"On you, you mean?"

"Jo, I didn't think it through."

"Clearly. And see, even though I liked Lauren and I believe you that you're not planning to get something romantic going with her again—"

"Jo. Hand to God. I would never do something like that to you, or to anyone I care about. Never, I promise you."

"Okay. I do believe you. But it does make me wonder what other secrets you're keeping. It makes me wonder if you'll do it again—hide something from me because you think telling me the truth is going to upset me somehow. Not telling me something like that is just lying by omission."

"I screwed up." He stood. "I see that. I'm sorry. I really am."

Her soft lips curved in a forced smile. "Okay."

He went to her, sat beside her and took her hand. "Jo. Please believe me. Lauren and me, we're over. So over. The truth is that it was never going to work with her and me. It was always you, Jo. I love…"

She stopped him with the light touch of her fingers against his lips. "Please don't."

"But I need you to know—"

"Uh-uh. Look. I'm not happy that you didn't tell me you had a meeting with your ex. But that's not the real problem here. I think you know it's not. The problem is the same one it's always been. You belong here. You would be a fool to walk away from all this. I saw you tonight, in your element, living the life that you love. But your life is not for me. I don't want to uproot my little girl. I don't want to leave my home, my family."

"But we can work it out. I know that we can. Just give me some time to—"

"No, Hunter. I don't think so. I really don't."

Now she was starting to piss him off. "So we're just going to give up and walk away? Is that what you're saying?"

"Wasn't that the plan all along?"

"Well, yeah, it was. I mean when we started."

"And since we got back together, nothing has changed."

"But it's not over yet. It's at least a month before the show wraps. There's still time."

"Time to what?"

He threw up both hands. "Be together. Work something out…"

"I don't know what we can work out. I really

don't. And I thought I could take it, that I could have this time with you and then walk away. But it's hurting too much already. So much that I really need to step back."

Okay, now. *This*. This was bad. "Step back?"

"Hunter, I need to get a little distance here."

"Distance." The word tasted like sawdust in his mouth. "From me, you mean?"

"Yeah." Her voice broke on that answer. "I do, Hunter. I need this to stop. It hurts too much, to be with you and know that we're just…what? Having fun, I guess. That it's going nowhere. That every day I get more and more attached, until I'm starting to feel like losing you is going to break me this time. I just… I can't do this anymore."

He looked in those unhappy eyes of hers and realized that he couldn't do it, either. Not when she couldn't see that they had options, that they really could make it work if they wanted it enough, if they both decided they belonged together and set out as a team to find a way.

But she refused to do that. She was giving up.

And it was a battle he couldn't fight all alone. He'd spent his childhood trying to fight the good fight for both him and his dad. It hadn't worked. He needed to learn his damn lesson here. It couldn't work, not when the woman he loved wouldn't even try.

"Alright then," he said.

"Um." Her voice cracked. "Alright, what?"

"It's over. I'll sleep in the other room."

Chapter Twelve

Sunday, Jo and Hunter avoided each other.

She spent half the day down on the beach. He climbed in his Porsche and drove away. She had no idea where he might have gone, but he stayed away until after she'd finished her solitary dinner. When he came in, she went upstairs to the bedroom suite he'd given her and didn't come out until early Monday morning.

The private jet to Sheridan took off at 10:00 a.m. Jo sat down first. Hunter walked right past her seat and settled on the other side of the plane.

Mel and David flew with them. The producer and the director took seats together but didn't talk much. Overall, the flight was eerily quiet.

Once, when Mel got up to use the restroom, she paused to hover over Jo's seat and asked way too cheerfully, "Everything okay?"

"Little headache," she lied. It was an awful, pounding, soul-crushing headache that very much included her broken heart. "Just resting."

"I have ibuprofen, if that might help."

"Already took some, thanks."

Mel patted her shoulder. "Well. Let us know if there's anything we can do."

"Thanks, Mel. 'Preciate it."

In Sheridan, Mel and David had a car and driver waiting. Hunter and Jo rode to the Rising Sun in his rented crew cab. The silence between them was absolute—that is, until Hunter turned onto Rising Sun land.

Then he said, "I'll pack up as soon as we get there and find a room in town."

Swallowing down a big knot, she nodded. "That'll work."

When they arrived at her house, everyone ran out of the main house to greet them. Jo put on a smile and got through it.

Her baby helped. Paisley cried, "Maw-maw-maw!" And reached out urgent arms. Jo took her. Paisley grabbed her around the neck and started sobbing.

Jo breathed in her sweet, milky scent and held her good and tight. "Now, now, baby," she whispered. "It's all right, Maw-maw's here, you know it's all right," she said while her mom and dad and Edna looked on, teary-eyed.

"Come on in the house." Tess put an arm around her and gave her a side-hug. "I've got coffee and dinner's all made—Hunter, you, too!"

"Thanks, but I've got to get going." He gave Tess a wave and a perfunctory smile as he carried his and Jo's suitcases into her house.

When the door shut behind him, Zach asked, "What's going on?"

Jo kissed her daughter's cheek, gulped down the threatening tears and tried to decide how to answer that question.

Her dad and her mom shared a speaking glance and then her dad said, "Never mind." He wrapped an arm around Jo from the other side and kissed her cheek the way she'd just kissed Paisley's— tenderly. With unwavering love.

Later, after dinner, her parents wanted to talk. She just couldn't go into it. Not right then. "I've really got to get moving," she said. "I need to un-pack. Decompress a little."

As always, they understood. After hugs all around, she took Paisley across the yard to her house, where her suitcase stood just inside the front door and all of Hunter's things were gone from her bedroom.

She waited until later, after Paisley was tucked

in her crib, sound asleep, to sit at the window in her bedroom—the one Hunter had climbed in that night back in May when they finally became lovers again.

Outside, the shadows were growing longer but the sky had yet to darken. She wondered how she would get through the night.

And all the nights to come.

Her whole body ached, like she'd been thrown off a horse and hit the ground without tucking and rolling. Leaning back in the chair, she forced herself to take slow breaths. It didn't help. The tears came, like a flood. They rolled down her cheeks, into her mouth, down her throat to the collar of her shirt. Her nose ran. She kept swiping the wetness away, but more only followed.

"Reow." DC landed hard on her lap. He was actually purring, for once.

But it didn't last. The minute she tried to cuddle him, he wriggled free and made for the door.

She watched him run off through a veil of tears as she silently promised herself that she would get through this. She'd lost Hunter before and survived. She could do it again.

A fresh wave of sobs doubled her over. This time felt every bit as bad as before—worse. Now she knew for certain that she would never really get over him. She would miss Hunter Bartley for the rest of her life.

* * *

In the days that followed, her family left her alone with her misery. They sent her worried, loving looks, but they kept their mouths shut, which she greatly appreciated.

She went on with her life as usual and tried to ignore the giant hole in her heart, taking Paisley to her mom's in the morning, working with her horses, pitching in moving cattle, checking wells and burning ditches. She ran the swather on the third cut of the alfalfa crop. She felt better out on the land, felt at home, and that gave her comfort.

Every day, she arrived at the main house by three in the afternoon to pick up Paisley. It was important, after all, that she spent lots of time with her daughter. Plus, it helped to have her little girl to care for, to keep in the front of her mind how much family and home really mattered.

Too bad that by Friday, five days after Hunter had taken his stuff and moved out, her family decided they'd left her alone long enough.

That afternoon when she went to get Paisley, her mom answered the door alone.

Jo put on a smile. "Just came for Paisley."

"Come on in, honey."

Jo hesitated on the threshold. "Mom. I really want to get on home." Her mom just stood there, looking at her so patiently. Jo tried again. "Where's Paisley?"

"Still sleeping. We'll get her up in a minute—but sweetheart, we haven't seen much of you these past few days. Stay for dinner, why don't you?"

Jo longed to flat-out refuse the invitation. But she couldn't hide from her own family forever.

And why was she hiding, anyway? Her mom, her dad, her brothers, her sister—Edna and the rest of the family. They were a good part of the reason she couldn't bear to follow Hunter to California.

Ground rules were required, though. "I don't want to talk about Hunter, okay?"

Her mother took a minute to reply. Finally, wearily, she nodded. "Fair enough. We just want to see you, to spend a little time with you."

They wanted more than that. They wanted her to open up about her aching heart. But she wouldn't. She couldn't. It hurt way too much already. Talking about it would just make it worse.

When Edna coyly mentioned that she'd run into Hunter in town, Jo replied, "Great. But we are not talking about Hunter now, are we?"

"Now, Jobeth, I only—"

"No," Jo's mom interrupted her friend in a soothing tone. "We are not talking about Hunter."

Edna sighed but let it be.

The rest of the meal went relatively well. Jo felt her dad's worried gaze on her more than once. But Zach Bravo never stuck his nose in where it wasn't welcome. He did not mention anything even vaguely related to the man Jo refused to discuss.

That night after she'd put Paisley to bed, Nick called.

She saw his name on the display and knew she shouldn't answer. But she *had* married him and sometimes she still felt guilty that she'd never loved him the way a woman ought to love her husband.

Against her own better judgment, she took the call. "What is it, Nick?"

"Hey, there. I heard that Hunter's no longer staying with you at the ranch and I—"

"Look. I don't want to talk to you. I don't know why I answered this call."

"Please, Jobeth. I've been sober for a month now, going to AA, working the steps. I would really like to get together with you. I need to make amends."

"Amends? You're kidding me. The first words out of your mouth were about Hunter. You only changed your tune when I said I didn't want to talk to you."

"But—"

"I wish you well. I hope you stay sober. But don't call me again. I mean that."

"Jobeth—"

"Goodbye." She disconnected the call and blocked him, after which she put her head in her hands and longed to be someone other than herself—someone who would never in a million years have gotten involved with a messed-up guy like Nick. Someone who could either pack up herself and her baby, and run off to LA to be with the love of her life...

Or learn how to be truly happy without him.

Starr showed up on Sunday afternoon.

Jo opened the door and laid down the law. "I'm not going to talk about it."

"Look what I've got." Starr held up a bottle of El Tesoro Blanco. "And that's not all." She raised the bottle in her other hand. "Tres Agaves margarita mix. It's organic. Delish."

"Aren't you nursing?"

"I pumped. It's fine. Cara's with Beau. We need to sit out on that back deck of yours and talk...or not talk. But there should definitely be margaritas."

Jo actually smiled. "Strangely, I am finding I have to agree."

They poured the tequila and margarita mix over ice and sat on the back deck. When Paisley woke from her nap, Jo set her up on the deck in her play yard and gave her a bunch of toys. She seemed happy in the shade of the deck cover, chewing on her stuffed elephant, getting up to her feet and staggering to the opposite side of the play yard, throwing her rattles around.

After a couple of margaritas, Jo did talk to her sister. She told her about the call from Nick.

"The nerve of that guy," growled her sister. "He's trouble. Stay away from him."

"I intend to. I blocked his number."

"A wise move."

After another margarita, Jo indulged herself in mourning the sudden end of her too-short reunion with Hunter. She explained that now she was just trying to get through the days. "Things will get better over time," she said, and tried really hard to believe it. "I know they will."

Starr neither argued nor agreed. She just listened.

When she got up to go, she said, "I see that the bunkhouse is finished."

"Yeah, it looks great. So what if all the hands have said they prefer to stay in their trailers?"

Starr laughed. "I'll bet Dad doesn't care."

"You would be right. He and Mom will use it as a guesthouse. There's talk that Grandma Elaine and Grandpa Austin will be staying there this Christmas."

"Really?" Starr was pleased. "That would be great. I keep meaning to arrange a family trip back east for a visit and never seem to get around to it. And before I go, I, uh…" She glanced away.

"What? Just say it."

"Well, I dropped in at the library during taping

Friday. Mel Huvey said they're actually on schedule. Taping should be concluded in mid-August. They'll all be headed back to LA then."

Three weeks, and Hunter would be gone.

Why did getting that news suck all the air right out of her lungs? It hurt just to drag in a breath, though she already knew he would be leaving soon—he might as well be gone already. She hadn't seen him since he dropped her off a week ago now.

And by her own choice, she wouldn't see him again. She'd broken it off with him so she could get busy getting over him.

Unfortunately, getting over Hunter wasn't going all that well so far.

"Aw, Jo…" Starr grabbed her, hugged her tight and crooned soothing words as Jo cried. "He's at the Statesman, the Buffalo Bill Suite," she announced before she said goodbye. "It's on the second floor, near the—"

"I know where it is, Starr." Her sixth-grade teacher, Mrs. Easterly, had taken the whole class for a tour of the Statesman. The Buffalo Bill Suite was the biggest suite of the five suites in the hotel. It had a spacious sitting room and a balcony overlooking Crystal Creek.

Starr added, "Mel said Hunter's there every night early. So if you wanted to talk to him some evening, chances are good you could catch him in his suite—and I know, you could so easily just call him. But sometimes it's better to take a man by surprise. Shows more initiative, and that you care enough to really put yourself out there."

"Ambush him, you mean?"

"It's only an ambush if you're bringing a gun."

"Starr! That is not even funny."

"Well, yeah, it kind of is—here." Starr handed her a tissue. "Dry your eyes and think about what I've said."

After her sister drove away, Jo wandered inside. She and Starr had moved the play yard into the main room and Jo had put Paisley in it again before walking Starr out. Now, her little girl was lying on her back, chewing on her toes and staring dreamily at the exposed ceiling trusses.

Jo sat on the sectional and thought about Los Angeles, about surfing at Zuma Beach and how she really would like to get to know Yalena better. How the more she stewed over the situation, the more possible it seemed that she and her daughter could make a life there.

Sometime in the last long week of suffering, life in LA had started to seem doable. She could come home anytime she wanted to, make it a priority that Paisley would see her grandma and grandpa often.

Last time Hunter left her, she'd let him go.

Maybe she needed to reconsider her choice here.

Maybe love mattered at least as much as her life on the Rising Sun.

Her dad chose the next day to come looking for her.

She was leaning on a fence rail beneath a sky dotted with wisps of clouds while Freckles and her filly, Dot, nibbled grass beneath a maple tree. Her dad stepped up beside her. Winston, who had trailed along behind him, flopped to the grass nearby.

"Dot's looking good," Zach said.

She nodded. "Calm-natured, like her mama." She turned her head and their eyes met. "Go ahead," she said flatly. "I'm listening."

He stared off toward that lone maple. "I've got a little speech all prepared."

"All right."

Her dad took a minute. They stared at the horses together. Finally, he began, "Since you were eight years old, I've known that you would be the one to step up, to take care of the Rising Sun when I'm gone. I've always felt a sense of peace about that. You were born for this. Ethan John and Brody will be there for you, whatever you need. Starr and your mom will always back you up. Cash and Nate and their families, too. But we all knew that when the time came, you would be running things. I don't want that to change."

"Me, neither." She couldn't look straight at him right now. If she did that, she wouldn't be able to keep it together. Instead, she focused on Freckles, watched her tail twitch and the wind tease her white-and-black mane as she nipped at the grass. "And Dad, I don't want to be taking over from you for a long, long time."

Her dad gave a slow nod. "No man can know when he will be called to account, but I'm thinking more than likely I've got several good years left."

She hooked her boot on the lower rail and leaned her head against his shoulder. "You better."

"What I'm saying is there's plenty of time for you to work things out with the man you love."

Jo closed her eyes and drew in a slow breath through her nose. "I would have to move to LA, me and Paisley."

"Well, if you did, that doesn't mean you'll always live in California. And for as long as you do, they have planes and cars to get us all back and forth to see each other often, no problem."

"Yeah." It came out in a whisper.

"Sometimes a person has to choose love over everything."

"Yeah. I see that."

"You tried the other way, Jo."

She swallowed a sob. "Last time, yeah."

"How'd that work out for you?"

"Dad. I was going to choose the Rising Sun again. I really was. I broke it off with him. But now…"

"You can't let him go without you."

"You're right. I can't."

"One thing I learned the hard way, Jo."

"What?"

"It's always better to put love first. Love is the best starting point. You get that right, everything else will fall into place."

For the rest of that day and the next few days, too, her dad's words echoed in her mind. Her dad had it right, as usual.

It was time to choose Hunter, time to go to him and say how wrong she'd been. To tell him she loved him, always had, always would. To ask him to take her and Paisley with him when he returned to LA.

She needed to reach out to him.

And yet, she failed to make her move.

At least twenty times a day, she pulled out her phone to call him. But then she would think of Starr's advice and decide that, no, she needed to get over to the Statesman that evening and show up at the door to his suite. It was a territorial hotel, with a wide, curving staircase rising up from the lobby to the second floor. Not like modern hotels, where you had to have a key card to access the floors with guest rooms.

She could get to him there, no problem. All she needed was the guts to make it happen.

Early Friday morning, as she fed her mother's chickens, Jo made her decision. She *had* to stop agonizing over Hunter and make her move. Tonight.

She would ask her mom to take Paisley. Then she would head for town. With a little luck, Hunter might even be there in his suite when she knocked on the door. If he was, she would tell him she loved him and *would* love him forever—and wouldn't he please take her and Paisley with him when he returned to LA?

Really, it was as good a plan as any.

She came in from the horse barn at five and went to the main house, where her mom hugged her and said, of course, she would keep the baby overnight. Jo kissed her little girl and ran back to her house to clean up and change into something irresistible before driving into town. She figured she had plenty of time. Even if he wasn't staying out partying all night, Hunter would still want dinner before heading for his suite. Seven would likely be a good time to catch him there.

She hoped.

But she felt so nervous, so unsure of herself right now. She dithered over what to wear, though dithering had never in her life been a problem for her. Tonight, though, nothing in her closet seemed like the exact right thing to make Hunter take one look at her and suddenly realize he couldn't live without her.

An hour after she left the main house, she stood barefoot in her bedroom, still dressed in her dusty T-shirt and jeans, trying to decide on the magic outfit that would change everything between her and the man she would never stop loving.

The doorbell rang.

"Coming!" She headed for the front door and got about halfway across the main room when her ex-husband emerged from the entry hall.

A strange, strangled sound escaped her at the sight of him. Halting in her tracks, she stood stock-still. Her mind just couldn't accept what her eyes were telling her.

Not Nick. No way. This can't be happening...

They faced off in the open space between the living area and the kitchen—Nick just beyond the entry hall and Jo beside her big farm-style kitchen table.

He'd been drinking. His cheeks were flushed, his eyes bloodshot. Sheepishly, he explained, "I rang the bell, but then the door was unlocked. So I just, y'know, let myself in."

After she'd kicked him out four years ago, she'd locked the door when she was home and whenever she left. But over time, she'd gotten lax about it.

Big mistake.

"Let yourself right back out," she instructed, her cool tone belying the fear that curled in her belly and the frantic racing of her heart. "Now."

He shook his head, his expression so sad and reproachful. "Come on, Jobeth…"

"I mean it, Nick. Please leave. Now."

"I jus' wanna talk. I *am* leavin', I promise you. Leavin' for good. After today, you won't be seeing me anymore."

"Honestly, Nick. We've got nothing to talk about. I'll say it again. Please go."

He braced his hands on his hips, pushing back his rumpled jacket in the process. She saw he had a pistol in a shoulder holster.

Her mouth got a coppery taste as her pulse slammed into high gear. Now the sound of her own heartbeat roared in her ears.

He saw the direction of her gaze and put up both hands. "Wait. No. I'm not here to hurt you. I jus'… Well, I ran into a li'l trouble in town and I have to get gone, but first I wanted to apologize—you know, make amends with you for…everything. Because amends are important. They are part of the process."

She could not bring herself to accept the weak-ass apology of a man who'd walked into her house without invitation carrying a gun under his jacket.

Moreover, she longed to point out that amends didn't work that way. You couldn't make amends while drunk, let alone when the person you were trying to make amends with had asked you to leave. Unfortunately, pointing out the flaws in Nick Collerby's reasoning on any given subject had never gone well for her.

Jo pressed her lips together and said nothing on the subject of making amends.

Nick said, "I want you to know I've always loved you, Jobeth. I jus' never did all that good of a job of it, now did I?"

Talk about an understatement. She sucked in a slow, calming breath through her nose and asked, "What kind of trouble are you in?"

He grunted. "The usual kind. Money trouble. But don't you worry 'bout that. Jobeth, I jus' need you to know that…" A vehicle pulled to a stop out in front. Nick blinked. "Someone's here." His eyes narrowed and he demanded furiously, "Who?"

She had no idea. "One of the hands, I would imagine, probably stopping by the main house. Really, I don't know."

They stared at each other. She heard the sound of a truck door shutting. He narrowed his eyes at her, not buying whatever he'd decided she was trying to sell him. "Don't lie to me, Jobeth."

"I'm not lying."

Someone mounted the front steps. Nick whirled toward the sound and then back on her. "Who's that?"

"I told you, I don't know. Just, please, stay calm and I'll get rid of whoever it is."

"Don't you even move, or I'll..." The chime of the doorbell cut him off in midthreat. Nick drew the pistol as he spun to face the door again.

Jo watched in horror as the door slowly swung open by itself—apparently, Nick had not engaged the latch.

It was Hunter. Nick muttered something under his breath...and fired.

Chapter Thirteen

Inside her own head, Jo was screaming.

But, in fact, she reacted without making a sound. The shot ringing in her ears, she grabbed a straight chair from its place at the table, raised it high and brought it down on Nick's head with enough force that one of the legs snapped off and rolled under the sectional sofa, where DC was lurking.

The cranky cat hissed in annoyance as Nick hit the floor like a safe.

The gun went spinning away from his limp hand. Hunter dipped to a crouch and caught it before it could whirl by him. Hardly daring to believe that he was still upright, she watched him engage the safety.

He glanced up and their eyes met. For a moment, they just stared at each other, frozen in place.

And then finally, her legs got the message from her brain. She ran to him. Careful of the weapon, he gathered her close in his warm arms, surrounding her with his strength and his longed-for woodsy scent.

She felt his lips in her hair as she asked in a ragged whisper, "Are you hit?"

He kissed her cheek. "Nope. You?"

"Not a scratch."

She glanced back at the man on the floor. "Looks to me like Nick's out cold."

"Looks to me like you're right," Hunter replied. Right then, she heard boots pounding up the front walk. Over Hunter's shoulder through the still-open front door, she spotted her dad as he ran up the steps, Winston at his heels.

Zach froze in the open doorway. The dog halted, too. "Jo?" Her dad's face was pale.

"We're both okay, Dad."

"Thank God. I was just across the yard. I saw Hunter drive up. I was halfway up the steps to the main house, trying to mind my own business, when I swear I heard a shot…"

Hunter had turned to face her dad, too. "Nick stopped by. With this pistol." He held up Nick's weapon. "He shot at me and missed, then Jo knocked him out with a chair."

"Thank God you're both still standing." Zach crossed the threshold and quietly shut the door behind him. Pausing only to clasp Jo's shoulder in reassurance, he went straight to the unconscious Nick. Winston followed him, keeping close. Kneeling, Zach pressed two fingers to the side of Nick's throat. After several too-quiet seconds, he said, "Pulse is steady and he's breathing normally."

Nick stirred, groaning. Winston growled.

"Sit, boy," Zach commanded. The dog dropped to his haunches. Zach took off his belt and bound Nick's hands behind his back. "I don't think he'll be causing anymore trouble today, but we might as well be on the safe side." A wry smile tugged on his lips. "By the way, good to see you, Hunter."

"Good to be back." Hunter slid Jo a look that was tender and hopeful and brimming with promise.

That look lit her up inside. All of a sudden, in her bare feet, dusty jeans and a wrinkled shirt, she felt like the most beautiful woman alive...and the luckiest, too. Nick was out of commission and she had Hunter at her side.

As for Hunter, he was feeling pretty good about everything, too, by then. He'd held Jo in his arms and just now, she'd smiled at him.

Her dad's phone rang. Zach pulled it from his

pocket and checked the display. "It's your mom," he said to Jo. Putting the phone to his ear, he spoke soothingly. "It's okay, sweetheart. I'm here, at Jo's… We're fine… Yes, you're right, you heard a shot… You did? Good… Yeah." As he stuck the phone back in his pocket, he explained, "Your mom says she heard the shot, too, and she's already called the sheriff's office. Someone should be here soon. Edna's there to look after Paisley, so your mom is coming right over."

Tess arrived a few minutes later. She grabbed Jo first and hugged her good and hard.

Then she turned to Hunter and laid her cool hand to the side of his face. "I am so glad to see you."

He almost choked up. "It's good to see you, too, Tess."

Quickly, she moved on to Zach for a kiss, after which she braced her fists on her hips and glared down at the groaning man on the floor. "Oh, Nick. What have you gotten yourself into now?"

Right then, they all heard the wail of a siren in the distance.

Two deputies arrived. They took statements. Eventually one of them escorted a handcuffed Nick out.

The other deputy gave Zach back his belt and collected the evidence, including Nick's pistol and the battered bullet that had ricocheted off the iron-work frame of the front door and landed on the floor of the entry hall.

Nick really was in serious trouble. He would be booked for unlawful entry, attempted murder, unlawful use of a firearm and aggravated assault.

Also, he'd embezzled a good deal of money from his father's insurance business. Beyond that, he'd been diverting insurance premiums into his own pockets and then failing to deliver the policies to the insurer. He'd denied a bunch of valid claims. Plus, he and Aida Ketchum were involved in a little side business staging car accidents.

"Nick Senior has had enough," said the talkative deputy before he went out the door. "No matter how lenient the judge at his arraignment turns out to be, I predict that Nick Junior will not be making bail—oh, and he left his vehicle down your driveway a hundred yards or so, out of sight of the houses. I'm going to go have a look at it right now and then we'll send a tow truck for it, so don't be surprised when the guy from A-1 Towing shows up."

"Thank you," Jo said as she ushered him out.

It was quiet once the chatty deputy left. The shock of what had happened lingered.

After a minute or two, Zach put his arm around Tess. "Close call," he said.

"Too close," Tess agreed.

"Come on over to the main house, you two." Zack smiled at Hunter and then at Jo. "Your mom's made her famous pot roast."

Tess grinned. "You don't want to miss that."

Hunter glanced at Jo and found she was already looking at him. "Thanks, Mom. Not tonight, though. But I do want to run over there and get Paisley." She gave her mom a wobbly smile. "I want her here, with us…"

Us. Damn. He really liked the sound of that.

Her mom and dad shared a look. Her mom said softly, "I'm not surprised. And I imagine you two have a lot to talk about."

"Yeah," said Hunter, his gaze locked with Jo's. "We do."

With Winston herding them all from behind, they trooped over to the other house, where the baby was sound asleep. When Jo picked her up, she hardly stirred.

Before they left, Edna gave Jo a hug—a careful one, so as not to wake the sleeping Paisley.

She turned to Hunter next and hugged him, too. "Breakfast nice and early," she said. "Hope you three will join us—and don't feel you have to say yes right now. The door is always open."

"Thank you," he replied as Jo stepped up to hug her mom and then Zack. Paisley, in the middle of those hugs, slept on.

Back at Jo's house, they went straight to the baby's room. "Here." Jo handed the little one to him.

Paisley's eyes popped open. "Hunh!" she said and gaped at him in surprise. Then, with a tiny sigh, she settled her head on his shoulder and went right back to sleep. Hunter rubbed her warm little back and thought how good it felt to hold her again.

"Okay," Jo whispered, after fussing with the blankets. "Put her to bed." Paisley went into her crib without a peep and Jo pulled the covers up over her.

Out in the main room, Jo turned and rested her hands on his chest. "I can't believe you're really here," she whispered, like it was a big secret, one she would never share with anyone else.

"Believe it." He pulled her close. "I missed you. So much…"

"Me, too…" She lifted her sweet mouth.

Their kiss was long and deep. His head swam and his body ached for her. When she sank back to her bare heels, she said, "I love, you Hunter. I was coming to look for you at the Statesman Hotel tonight. But then Nick showed up before I could decide what to wear to wow you so hard you would have to agree to take me and Paisley with you to California when you go."

Damn. He might just be the happiest man on the

planet at this moment. She loved him. She'd said it right out loud. "You are so beautiful."

She scoffed. "In bare feet and dirty work clothes with my hair all over the place?"

"Yep. You're my dream girl—always have been. I love you, Jobeth. There's no one else for me."

She kissed him again. And then she asked, "Hungry?"

He was. She took his hand and led him around the overturned one-legged chair and into the kitchen, where she made them a couple of fat roast beef sandwiches with lettuce, tomato and horse-radish sauce. He grabbed a bag of chips and a couple of beers from the fridge.

"Take the baby monitor," she said.

He rearranged the stuff in his hands and grabbed the monitor off the counter. They went out to the back deck, where they sat at the little iron table with the two café chairs.

They ate without saying much. Right then, words seemed unnecessary. He was where he needed to be and she seemed glad to have him there.

When they'd finished the food, she stacked their plates and set the half-empty chip bag on top of them.

After a last sip of her beer, she put down the empty bottle carefully. "I want to be with you. I want a life with you. I've thought long and hard on how to make that happen and, well, I'm hoping you'll agree to take me and Paisley back to LA with you when you go."

He shook his head. "Jo…"

"Hunter, please. Don't look at me with doubt. I know what I'm doing. I've gone over and over this choice, believe me. And Hunter, I'm ready to put you first. I wasn't before, that's the sad truth."

"It's okay."

"No, it's not. I was…damaged, as you already know, by the life we had, my mom and me, before we came to Medicine Creek. I mean, my birth dad wasn't a bad guy. Looking back now, I see he just had this hunger in him to make it big at any cost.

"I was just a little kid, but I knew Mom was scared a lot, that we couldn't pay our bills, that we were always moving, sometimes sneaking away in the middle of the night so the landlord wouldn't demand the back rent…"

"You just wanted a home," he said quietly. "You wanted to stay in one place, not to be always moving, starting over somewhere new and strange."

"Exactly. And then my dad died and we came to Wyoming—at first, to live with Edna in town."

"And you loved it."

She gave him a wistful little grin. "You know this story as well as I do."

"That's right," He knew because she'd told him

this story more than once back when they were first together. "You moved in with Edna and you never wanted to leave."

"And the first time we came out here to the Rising Sun, I just knew that I'd found home at last." She met his eyes across the small table. "I didn't realize then what I finally know now. Hunter, now I see that *you* are my home."

"Jo…" He wanted to grab her, hold her, promise her the world and swear he would never, ever leave her again.

But she had more to say. "I want a life with you. When I get desperate for the Rising Sun, I'll come back for a visit. We can figure it out, day by day. But the main thing, the important thing, is that we're together."

He caught her hand and pressed his lips to the back of it. "I don't know where to start."

She swallowed, hard. "Say yes."

"But see, Jo, I haven't been completely honest with you…"

She gasped and snatched her hand away. "What? Tell me. Tell me this instant, Hunter Bartley. What's going on?"

"Hey, now. Slow down. It's not bad, it's good."

She peered at him, frowning. "You haven't been completely honest—and that's good, how?"

"It's just that I haven't told you everything. I've

been working it out, that's all. I want to be with you, too, however we can make that happen. I know you love this land and this town. And you already know that since coming back to Medicine Creek, I've learned that I got a lot of things wrong when we were kids, that this is my hometown, too. That I want to be here. And more than just wanting to be here, Jo, I want to be here with you."

She drew a shaky breath. Her blue eyes shone with unshed tears. "You mean that?"

"I do. With all my heart. And the reason I haven't told you everything is because I didn't want to get ahead of myself. I wanted to come to you with more than just promises. I needed a plan."

"Wait. There's a plan?"

"There is, yeah."

She jumped to her feet…and then plopped right back down in her chair again. "Tell me!"

"First, I just want to say again that, as far as Lauren goes, I only met with her because I thought she and I might put together a project that would make it possible for me to keep my career somehow and stay here in Wyoming, too…with you. But her offer wasn't workable."

"Not workable, how?"

"The show she's developing is called *Vacation Renovation*. I would be fixing up people's vacation homes all over the world. I should have just told you upfront that I was meeting with her, but I didn't know what she was going to offer at that point, so I thought I would wait to tell you about it until I knew what the deal was. And then it was nothing I wanted to do, so I said nothing to you."

She regarded him solemnly. "Yes. And you were wrong not to tell me, Hunter."

"You're right. And I got what I deserved— which is busted—when she showed up at Terry's party to try again to get me on board."

"Just tell me the truth. Are you still thinking of working with her?"

"No! That deal is a no-go. I'm just explaining why I met with her in the first place. I'm apologizing for not telling you what I was up to and I'm promising you that I will never pull any crap like that again."

She let out a slow breath. "You are forgiven. And I have to say, I'm glad that whatever her deal was, you didn't take it. I would try really hard not to be jealous if you were going to be working with her. But you and your ex-wife working together, well, that would not be my choice, you know?"

"Jo."

"Hmm?"

"She's not you. The whole time I was married to her, I felt lonely. I thought of you constantly. I wondered if I would ever feel the way I felt with you again. It was always about you."

"Yeah?" The question came out in a husky whisper.

"Yeah. And I swear to you. Lauren and I really are over."

"I believe you. I truly do."

"And I will *never* be working with her again."

Jo laughed then. "Hey. Never's a big word and you two are in the same industry. But I can't help feeling relieved that you won't be working with her in the near future."

"I won't be—and the real news is that I *do* have a new deal in the works with Terry. See, there's a lot of buzz behind *Hunter Comes Home*. Focus groups love the family angle—the whole hometown concept. Terry thinks it grounds me, that I'm ready to move on from being a single guy putting in yet another new kitchen in some rich person's house. So we're going to refocus the show. We're going to build on the whole community aspect we've developed here in Medicine Creek, put the emphasis on family, on my life here in my hometown."

She blinked. "Okay, wait. You don't live here in your hometown."

"That's going to change. We're planning on basing the show right here. We would take on more projects in town, maybe in Sheridan and Buffalo, too. I would travel, yes, but just to nearby towns at first, with the possibility of eventually branching out into Montana, Colorado and Idaho. Yeah, there would still be time spent in LA—mostly in a business sense, meetings and planning sessions, networking, all that. But my base would be here in Wyoming."

She sat up a little straighter. "Here in Wyoming, with Paisley and me?"

"Oh, Jo. I hope so—if that works for you."

Her eyes were shining now. "We could live here most of the time, then, right here on the Rising Sun?"

"Yes, we could. I *want* to live here, with you."

"And Paisley and me, we could come with you, if you have to be in LA, or wherever?"

"Yes. Anytime, all the time, whenever you can. I love you, Jo. It's been so bad, these past two weeks since we broke up. I was just about to come here and beg you to be with me. I was just going to quit my show and move back to Medicine Creek, start fresh, the two of us—and I promise, if that's how you want it, that's how it will be."

"Hunter, I never wanted you to give up your show."

"I'm just saying it's an option."

"No way. That's not right."

He put up a hand. "Well, as it turns out, I got the call from Terry this afternoon confirming that the plan was a go. I drove like a bat out of hell as soon as we finished filming today, to get to you, to beg you to give me another chance, to tell you that I just want to make it work for us. I want you and me together. Jo, whatever we decide, I just want to be with you. I don't think I can bear to lose you all over again."

"Oh, Hunter, I know *I* couldn't bear it." She jumped to her feet. And this time, she scooted around the table, plunked down in his lap and wrapped her arms around his neck. "Yes. To all of it, including your new deal with Terry Sloane. Let's do it, let's go for it—because whatever happens, Hunter Bartley, wherever life takes us, I want us to be going there together, you and me and Paisley, too."

"Yes."

Grabbing the collar of his shirt, she yanked him close and crashed her mouth to his in a frantic, hungry, perfect kiss.

He could have kissed her forever, but he had more he needed to say. Taking her by the waist, he rose and set her down on her bare feet.

She still had her arms twined good and tight around his neck. "Get back here. Kiss me again."

"You bet I will. But first…"

"No, no! First comes kissing. A lot of kissing. I've missed you so much and I can't wait another minute to…" Her protests died in the cutest little squeak of surprise as he dropped to one knee. "Hunter! What are you doing?"

He stuck his hand in his pocket and pulled out the antique ring he'd found in the old pine nightstand next to his father's bed several days after Esau Bartley went fishing for the last time. The square-cut aquamarine stone was flanked by diamonds in a platinum band.

"It was my mother's." His voice came out rough and low. "My grandma Daisy once told me that my dad found it at an estate sale years and years ago. He paid a lot for it. He wanted the perfect engagement ring for my mom, so he bought it. I've kept it all this time. I always knew that it was meant to be yours, though for years I was afraid you would never wear it."

"Oh, Hunter. It's so beautiful…"

He took her left hand. "Marry me, Jo. Let's make it forever. I love you. I will always love you. There is no one but you—then, now and always."

"Oh! Oh, I can't even…"

"Just say yes."

She smiled then as tears welled in her eyes. "Yes!"

He slipped the ring on her finger and swept to his feet to gather her close.

"I love you," she whispered.

"And I love you."

"It's you and me, Hunter, from now on. No matter what happens, what difficulties get in our way, we are together. Unbreakable. A team. Promise me that."

"I promise, Jo. This is really happening. This is finally the start of our forever."

"Yes! Now kiss me."

And he did, sweetly at first and then with increasing fervor. He kissed her and went on kissing her as he gathered her high in his arms and turned to carry her inside through the back door and straight to her room.

Setting her down on the rug by the bed, he got to work stripping off his clothes.

"Come back here." She grabbed his arm and pulled him close again for another endless, perfect kiss.

Out in the grassy pasture behind the house, a meadowlark burst into song. Somewhere in the wide sky above, a red-tailed hawk let out its hoarse, eerie cry as it soared on the wind.

As for Hunter Bartley, he was where he needed most to be—home at last in Jobeth Bravo's loving arms.

From the Medicine Creek Clarion,
week of August 20
Over the Back Fence
by
Mabel Ruby

It was an outdoor wedding for Jobeth Bravo and Hunter Bartley just this past Saturday, August 19, at the Bravo family ranch, the Rising Sun. The Reverend Marilee Ramirez presided beneath a cloudless blue sky as the happy couple vowed to love, honor and cherish one another for the rest of their lives.

After the ceremony, the bride, the groom, the bride's precious little one, their families, a large group of friends and the entire cast and crew of the groom's hit TV show, *Rebuilt by Bartley*, celebrated with a big barbecue, live music and dancing under the stars. It was after eleven at night when the bride and groom cut the towering ten-tiered wedding cake.

The groom, recently returned to Medicine Creek after years pursuing his successful career in Los Angeles, will be settling down with his bride at the Rising Sun Ranch.

Jobeth and Hunter, may we take this opportunity to wish you both health, wealth, love and happiness as you set forth on the great adventure known as married life!

* * * * *

*Watch for Tyler Ross Bravo's story
coming in December 2023, only
from Harlequin Special Edition*

#2971 FORTUNE'S FATHERHOOD DARE
The Fortunes of Texas: Hitting the Jackpot • by Makenna Lee
When bartender Damon Fortune Maloney boasts that he can handle any kid, single mom Sari Keeling dares him to watch her two rambunctious boys for just one day. It's game on, but Damon soon discovers that parenthood is tougher than he thought—and so is resisting Sari.

#2972 HER MAN OF HONOR
Love, Unveiled • by Teri Wilson
Bridal-advice columnist and jilted bride Everly England couldn't have predicted the feelings a sympathetic kiss from her best friend would ignite in her. Henry Aston knows the glamorous city girl is terrified romance will ruin their friendship. But this stand-in groom plans to win her "I do" after all!

#2973 MEETING HIS SECRET DAUGHTER
Forever, Texas • by Marie Ferrarella
When nurse Riley Robertson brought engineer Matt O'Brien to Forever to meet the daughter he never knew he had, she was only planning to help Matt see that he can be the father his little girl needs. But could the charming new dad be the man Riley didn't know she needed? And are the three ready to become a forever family?

#2974 THE RANCHER'S BABY
Aspen Creek Bachelors • by Kathy Douglass
Suddenly named guardian of a baby girl, rancher Isaac Montgomery gamely steps up for daddy duty, with the help of new neighbor Savannah Rogers. Sparks fly, but Savannah's reserved even as their feelings heat up. Are Isaac and his baby too painful a reminder of her heartbreaking loss? Or do they hold the key to healing?

#2975 ALL'S FAIR IN LOVE AND WINE
Love in the Valley • by Michele Dunaway
Unexpectedly back in town, Jack Clayton is acting as if he never crushed Sierra James's teenage heart. When he offers to buy her family's vineyard, the former navy lieutenant knows Jack is turning on the charm, but no way is she planning to melt for him again. But will denying what she still feels for Jack prove to be a victory she can savor?

#2976 NO RINGS ATTACHED
Once Upon a Wedding • by Mona Shroff
Fleeing her own nuptials wasn't part of wedding planner Sangeeta Parikh's plan. Neither was stumbling into chef Sonny Pandya's arms and becoming an internet sensation! So why not fake a relationship so Sangeeta can save face and her job, and to get Sonny much-needed exposure for his restaurant? It's a good plan for two commitmentphobes...until their fake commitment starts to feel all too real.

YOU CAN FIND MORE INFORMATION ON UPCOMING HARLEQUIN TITLES, FREE EXCERPTS AND MORE AT HARLEQUIN.COM.

HSECNM0223

Get 4 FREE REWARDS!

We'll send you 2 FREE Books plus 2 FREE Mystery Gifts.

FREE
Value Over
$20

Both the **Harlequin® Special Edition** and **Harlequin® Heartwarming™** series feature compelling novels filled with stories of love and strength where the bonds of friendship, family and community unite.

HARLEQUIN
PLUS

Try the best multimedia subscription service for romance readers like you!

Read, Watch and Play.

Experience the easiest way to get the romance content you crave.

Start your **FREE TRIAL** at
<u>www.harlequinplus.com/freetrial</u>.